They'd kissed.

Once, at a party in the second year of Hope's studies. They'd laughed that off as the kind of thing everyone did at Christmas parties, and when she'd gone home for Christmas, Hope's father had died suddenly. When it became obvious that her mother couldn't cope alone, Hope had transferred to a medical school closer to home. The kiss had been forgotten.

Only, somehow, Hope could almost taste it on her lips. Maybe because of the look in Theo's dark eyes...

"You know each other?" Sara Jamieson never much liked being out of the loop.

"We were at medical school together for a while. Theo was a few years ahead of me." Hope had to admit that he was wearing those years well. "We haven't seen each other for..."

"Eighteen years." Theo grinned. Apparently their old habit of finishing each other's sentences hadn't reached its expiry date yet.

Hope got to her feet, staring at Theo, which was okay because he was staring at her. He wasn't quite the same. His dark hair had a streak of gray at the temples and his manner was a little more self-assured. But he still had that certain something that had drawn Hope to him and not allowed her to forget that kiss.

Dear Reader,

I suppose I'm like a lot of people in saying that some of the plans and dreams I had in my early twenties have been realized and some haven't. And that in hindsight I'm very relieved that several of them never did get past the drawing board stage. :)

Hope and Theo were good friends at medical school but haven't seen each other for nearly twenty years. In that time, Theo has had the chance to follow his dreams. But Hope's life has taken a different turn, and she feels that she's never been able to fulfill any of the plans she had for the future. They're both at a crossroads in their lives, wanting and needing different things, but now that they've found each other again, it's becoming increasingly difficult to let go.

Maybe this is the time for them to both realize that there's no age limit on new and different plans for the future. And that those plans can include each other if that's what they really want.

Thank you for reading Theo and Hope's story—I hope you enjoy it.

Annie x

THE GP'S SEASIDE REUNION

ANNIE CLAYDON

MEDICAL ROMANCE

Harlequin®
MEDICAL ROMANCE

Recycling programs
for this product may
not exist in your area.

ISBN-13: 978-1-335-94289-0

The GP's Seaside Reunion

Copyright © 2025 by Annie Claydon

All rights reserved. No part of this book may be used or reproduced in any manner whatsoever without written permission.

Without limiting the author's and publisher's exclusive rights, any unauthorized use of this publication to train generative artificial intelligence (AI) technologies is expressly prohibited.

This is a work of fiction. Names, characters, places and incidents are either the product of the author's imagination or are used fictitiously. Any resemblance to actual persons, living or dead, businesses, companies, events or locales is entirely coincidental.

For questions and comments about the quality of this book, please contact us at CustomerService@Harlequin.com.

TM and ® are trademarks of Harlequin Enterprises ULC.

Harlequin Enterprises ULC
22 Adelaide St. West, 41st Floor
Toronto, Ontario M5H 4E3, Canada
www.Harlequin.com

Printed in U.S.A.

Cursed with a poor sense of direction and a propensity to read, **Annie Claydon** spent much of her childhood lost in books. A degree in English literature followed by a career in computing didn't lead directly to her perfect job—writing romance for Harlequin—but she has no regrets in taking the scenic route. She lives in London, a city where getting lost can be a joy.

Books by Annie Claydon

Harlequin Medical Romance

Christmas North and South

Neurosurgeon's IVF Mix-Up Miracle

Greek Island Fling to Forever
Falling for the Brooding Doc
The Doctor's Reunion to Remember
Risking It All for a Second Chance
From the Night Shift to Forever
Stranded with the Island Doctor
Snowbound by Her Off-Limits GP
Cinderella in the Surgeon's Castle
Children's Doc to Heal Her Heart
One Summer in Sydney
Healed by Her Rival Doc
Country Fling with the City Surgeon
Winning Over the Off-Limits Doctor

Visit the Author Profile page
at Harlequin.com for more titles.

CHAPTER ONE

THE EXPECTED KNOCK on the door came at ten past eight. Dr Hope Ashdown looked up from her desk, a welcoming smile already forming on her lips. Dr Jamieson, the senior partner of Arrow Lane Medical Centre, had mentioned that the doctor who'd be filling in while Dr Anna Singh was on maternity leave would be starting work today.

'Meet Dr Lewis…' Sara Jamieson was clearly busy this morning, and taking the orientation tour at breakneck speed. Dr Lewis had better keep up or the chance for the briefest of hellos, or even a swift looking-forward-to-working-with-you, would be missed.

'Dr…' The word died on Hope's lips as the new doctor caught up, appearing in the doorway.

'Theo?'

'Hope!'

What were the chances? Recognising someone that you hadn't seen for eighteen years, straight away. Having them recognise you back and, against all the odds, remember your name… Hope couldn't calculate the exact likelihood of that, and settled for *highly unlikely*.

She'd been in the third year of her medical degree, and a little lost in the complexities of a large teaching hospital. Theo had been three years ahead of her, in the first year of his foundation training, and part of a scheme that helped third-year students make the transition from non-clinical to clinical study. He'd come to her rescue, tipping her off about the best way to approach the lead consultants on each of her rotations and telling her what to read up on to impress.

They'd become friends, and…they'd kissed. Once, at a Christmas party in the fourth year of Hope's studies. They'd laughed that off as the kind of thing everyone did at Christmas parties, and when she'd gone home for the holidays, Hope's father had died suddenly. She'd postponed her return in the new year and when it had become obvious that her mother couldn't cope alone, Hope had transferred to a medical school closer to home. They'd corresponded a lot at first, but slowly she'd felt she had less and less in common with Theo and their texts and messages had petered out. The kiss had been forgotten.

And she'd felt forgotten too, because Theo hadn't come to rescue her this time. She'd been mired in loss and regret, slowly coming to terms with the idea that her mother was going to need ongoing care and that all of her own plans needed to be put on hold for the foreseeable future.

But, somehow, Hope could still taste his kiss. Maybe because of the look in Theo's dark eyes…

'You know each other?' Sara Jamieson never much liked being out of the loop, and Hope smiled up at her.

'We were at medical school together for a while. Theo was a few years ahead of me.' Hope had to admit that he was wearing those years well. 'We haven't seen each other for...'

'Eighteen years.' Theo smiled. Apparently their old habit of finishing each other's sentences hadn't reached its expiry date yet.

'Well... Should I leave you to catch up? I have a few phone calls to make.' Sara clearly needed to be somewhere else at the moment.

'Yes. Thanks, Sara, I'll finish showing Theo around.'

Sarah flashed Hope a smile and hurried from the room. Hope got to her feet, staring at Theo, which was okay because he was staring at her. He wasn't quite the same, his dark hair had a streak of grey at the temples, and his manner was a little more measured. But he still had that certain something. Her head couldn't quantify it, but her thumping heart seemed to know just what it was.

Then he broke the silence. 'Is Dr Jamieson always that brusque?'

'No. She usually has a great deal of time for everyone here, and I imagine those phone calls she needs to make are urgent ones, on a patient's behalf.'

Theo nodded. 'I wish she'd mentioned it. I would have been more than happy to find my way around the place and introduce myself.'

Hope sat down, waving him towards the seat on

the other side of her desk, and he settled into it. Still staring at him, as if taking her eyes off him for one moment would make him disappear.

'I'm sorry I didn't keep in touch, Hope.'

That was Theo all over. Taking the initiative and saying the things she didn't dare say.

'It takes two to lose touch. I should apologise too.'

Suddenly, everything came flooding back, more potent than it had been before because Hope didn't take it for granted, now. The exchanged looks that told them both they were thinking the same thing. The warmth that didn't need words.

'It takes one to keep in touch.' He grinned at her.

'Then I suppose we'll both have to share the blame,' Hope shot back at him. 'It was a long time ago, Theo.'

She didn't want to think about it any more. He'd just walked back into her life and she wanted the adventurous pleasure of his smile. That still had the power to put the everyday humdrum of regret behind her for a while.

He nodded. 'So. What have you been up to in the last eighteen years? In three sentences or less...' Theo's tone intimated that he expected that to be a challenge.

Two sentences would probably cover it, just as long as she didn't try to justify not getting around to all of the things she'd planned to do. 'You remember I came back here to be near my mum?'

Theo nodded. 'How are things there?'

'Mum needed a lot of support after my dad died. She had a number of medical issues and never really got back on her feet again. She developed symptoms of dementia soon after I qualified as a doctor, so I moved in and looked after her until she died, four months ago.'

That covered it. Hope was staring the big four-zero in the face, and that was all she had to say about her life so far.

'I'm so sorry to hear that. It's a special kind of achievement, building a career and caring for someone.'

It was a nice thing to say. Hope gave a small shrug and Theo raised an eyebrow.

'You don't think so? You made a difference for your mum and she was lucky to have you.'

Making a difference had always been the highest praise that Theo could give. Eighteen years ago, he'd been sure that working in the community was his way of making that difference. Hope doubted that his path from there to here had been quite as straight and uneventful as hers had been.

'How about you, then? Eighteen years in three sentences.' She threw the question back at him, knowing that Theo couldn't resist a challenge.

'I trained for general practice, then decided to specialise in addiction issues, which have taken me abroad for most of the last fifteen years. I was married for a while, but it didn't last. My daughter has a university place in Brighton, and so I'm looking to establish a home base back in the UK now.'

'Wait…' Travel. Marriage. A child. Clearly the last eighteen years had been more eventful for Theo, and Hope wasn't sure which to ask about first. 'You have a daughter?'

'I've had my three sentences, haven't I?' Theo grinned.

'Your rules. You can break them.'

He nodded. Theo still had that streak of mischief running through his veins, and the thought sent shivers running down Hope's spine. 'Willow was twelve when I married her mother, and when she was thirteen she agreed to my adopting her formally. Carrie and I had talked about setting up home here in England after we got married, but she said she wanted more from life and was keen to travel. It turned out that I couldn't give her the *more* she wanted, because she found someone else and moved on, leaving me and Willow behind.'

'You sound bitter.' Hope hadn't meant to be that forthright, but it came so easily with Theo. He shrugged, puffing out a breath.

'Nah. Not for myself, at any rate. But Carrie shouldn't have walked out on Willow like that, and she was terrified. It took me a while to convince her that she didn't get rid of me so easily. She dropped behind with her schoolwork, but she worked hard and made that up. We were in Kenya for her gap year and then she landed a really good place at university and we came back to England two years ago. I did my GP's return to practice course up in London, and…here I am. Being here in Hastings is perfect for me, not too far from Willow if she needs me, and not so close that she feels I'm crowding her.'

His face was shining with pride. Theo had been there for his daughter when she'd needed him, and now he was going through the process of letting go. Hope had done her share of letting go, and Theo seemed to be making a better job of it than she was.

'So where have you been, for work?'

'Europe, Asia, Africa… The challenges are different in different places, but the answers are surprisingly similar.'

'And what made you decide on those challenges?' This was beginning to sound as if she were subjecting him to a second interview. 'I'm just interested. You never mentioned specialising in addiction issues at medical school.'

His face darkened. 'You remember Andrew Locke?'

'Of course I do. You and he were close friends, weren't you?'

'Yes, we were. And yet I missed all the signs, the same as everyone else did. A year after you left, he wrapped his car around a tree and was killed instantly. Toxicology showed that he had a high level of cocaine in his system.'

Hope's hand flew to her mouth. 'Andrew? He's the last person… Had he been taking drugs for long?'

'None of us thought he'd been taking them at all. That was the hardest thing—he had a lot of people who cared about him, but he'd never told anyone. His family were just as shocked as we were and we got together to try and find out what had happened. It turned out that he'd been using cocaine for almost three years, and that he'd been forging signatures on prescriptions to finance his habit. I got involved with a charity that aims to help people in the early stages of substance abuse—hopefully before their lives start to fall apart. I realised very quickly that I'd found my vocation.'

It was a lot to take in. *Theo* was a lot to take in. So much like the young man she'd known, and yet somehow more. A little more assured, maybe, but his dark eyes still glimmered with endless possibilities.

'How about you? You have a significant other? Or children?' Theo asked.

That would have been nice. Hope's parents had married relatively late in life, and she'd been their only child. There had been a lot of love in their small family, but she'd lost her father too early, and then found herself looking after her ailing mother. Hope had returned home willingly, but it felt a little as if the opportunity for making her own life had passed her by.

'I never really had the time. Dating's not that easy when you have to be home by seven because that's when Mum's daycare finishes.'

Theo nodded. He seemed to understand, although he couldn't possibly know all of it. The large house, full of secrets. Boxes upon boxes of things, which now made clearing the place and moving on an insurmountable task. But suddenly it seemed that there *was* a new life out there, even if it couldn't break through the all too physical barriers that had separated her home life from the world outside, ever since she was a child.

'You know Hastings?' She tried to make the question sound casual.

'I know my way from where I'm staying to here. And back out to the motorway, in case I ever need to escape. Since we're old friends, I was wondering whether you might give me a map reference for your favourite restaurant, so that I can buy you dinner sometime and quiz you on some of the best places to go.'

Theo had ticked all of the boxes. A dinner invitation could be many different things, but the addition of *old friends* and *sometime* put everything in its right place.

'That sounds good. How about next Saturday? We can take a stroll around the Old Town or along the seafront first.'

Theo's broad smile spoiled it all, by reminding Hope once again that she was a woman, and he was a very desirable man. 'I'd really like that. And in the meantime, if you could show me the way to my desk...'

In Theo's experience, moving on had always provided perspective, allowing him to cope with the pressures of a high-stress job. But seeing Hope again had been the exception to that rule. Everything he'd felt eighteen years ago was still sharp and clear, preserved unchanged through the passage of time, and it had hit him like a sledgehammer.

Her green eyes were still captivating, and her auburn hair shimmered in the sunshine, even if it was shorter now and her curls a little neater. He could feel the warmth of all the good times they'd had together, and the sharp pain of his heart breaking when she'd left. The realisation that he'd been a little in love with her had come too late, and the one kiss they'd shared had become the last of a whole catalogue of missed chances.

It had been a shock to see Hope again, but Theo had somehow managed to distance himself from the moment. He couldn't help his questions, though, or the careful probing for some hint that she'd been happy.

Neither of them were kids any more, starting out on an adventure that couldn't possibly fail. He'd had his share of bad times and Theo was in no doubt that Hope had, too, but he had no regrets.

He'd loved his work, even though there was a high failure rate, and the pain of his broken marriage was long gone. Willow had been an unexpected but precious gift.

And now he was back in England, starting again. An old friend had asked him to take his son on as a patient, and when the young man had died the family's grief had broken Theo. He'd returned to general practice, and somehow life had brought him around full circle. Seeing Hope had suddenly made him feel the thrill of an unknown future, beckoning him on.

Maybe Hope would understand that and maybe not. Her neat consulting room, decorated with plants and pictures, felt so different from the string of anonymous workplaces he'd inhabited over the years. She showed him to a room, just along the corridor from hers, opening the blinds to let the sunlight in.

There was a large desk, the surface clear except for a computer and telephone. A comfortable chair for him to sit in, along with patient seating and a curtained area that contained a couch. Everything was clean and tidy, and Hope looked around, wrinkling her nose.

'I think we can do a little better than this.' She marched through the open doorway, leaving him to look around and try the chair out for size. Then she reappeared, holding a couple of potted plants, which Theo guessed were from the exuberant greenery in her own consulting room.

'Will these do?'

Theo couldn't help smiling. Hope could always be trusted to bring a little colour to a room. 'They're great. Sure you won't miss them?'

She shook her head. 'You'll be doing me a favour. It takes me ages to water them all. Has someone given you a log-in for the computer system?'

'Not yet.' Theo took the plants from her, arranging them carefully on the deep windowsill behind him, as if they were precious jewels.

'I'll see if our practice manager knows.' Hope leaned over, picking up the telephone handset and dialling. 'Rosie, I'm with Dr Lewis. I don't suppose you know whether anyone's created a user profile for him on the system yet?'

She listened for a moment, quirking her mouth down. 'Oh. Okay, I'll tell him. Thanks…'

'What's the verdict?' Theo couldn't help grinning at her as she replaced the phone in its cradle.

'Well… Our IT guy will be here in an hour, and he's not allowed to give your password to anyone but you. And in the meantime, you're on vaccinations. The practice nurse usually does them but there are a lot to get through and she needs a hand.'

'Sounds good. I'll make a list.' Theo opened the top drawer of the desk, and found that it was empty.

'That's okay. Rosie's already printed out the list.

She's ferociously efficient, and if there's anything you ever want to know, she's your first port of call. I'll get you a pen, and you can ask her to show you the stationery cupboard when you get a moment. That's as long as she hasn't beaten you to it and already brought you everything you'll ever need.' Hope frowned. 'Sorry there isn't anything more exciting to do on your first morning.'

'Vaccinations can be exciting. Remember that bag of oranges you found yourself in a life-or-death struggle with?' Maybe she didn't. He shouldn't expect those memories to be as clear in Hope's mind as they were in his.

'You'll be happy to know I've improved a bit since then. No thanks to you and your "mad scientist" impressions, I'll have you know...'

She *did* remember. Better than he did. 'I'd forgotten all about those. Not very tactful on my part...'

'I survived.' Hope grinned, looked round as the practice manager appeared, holding a sheaf of paper. She ducked out of the room while Rosie took him through the list, explaining that he just needed to add his initials, the date and the batch number for each patient.

'Thanks, Rosie. Where can I find...?' Theo smiled as Hope reappeared in the doorway, holding up several brightly coloured pens. 'Ah. Never mind.'

Rosie looked round and rolled her eyes. 'I could

bring you something from the stationery cupboard, if you'd prefer grey?'

Hope chuckled at the thought, and Theo shook his head. 'Nothing says *welcome* quite like a hand-ful of pink pens.'

'Fair enough. I'll leave you to it, then. Extension 204 if you want anything.' Rosie shot Hope a smile on her way out of the room.

'You could have blue…' Hope's green eyes were daring him to stick with the pink.

'Nah. Blue's so mad-scientisty.' Suddenly Theo *was* at home. He had plants, and pens and an extension number to call. And Hope, to share jokes and memories with.

She nodded. 'True. Well, I'm within scream-ing distance so if I hear any cries for help, I'll be right back…'

CHAPTER TWO

BREATHLESS. IF SHE'D had any warning of Theo's arrival then Hope might have predicted a whole assortment of reactions, but there had been only one. She felt breathless.

Not the painful wheeze that she listened out for when examining a patient, or the panicky gasp for oxygen when life suddenly threw too much at her. This was as if she'd suddenly been set free, and could stretch and run again.

Hope sat in her consulting room, waiting for her next patient to make their way from the waiting room. The stretching and running were probably all an illusion—nothing had really changed and Theo had just reminded her of a time when she'd been young and thought that anything was possible. She turned down her mouth, reaching for the phone as it started to ring.

'Hope...' Rosie was muttering quietly, clearly not wanting to be overheard. 'Theo's finished the vaccination list, and the IT guy's given him access to the system. Can I get him to see Mrs Patel?'

'Yes, of course. She's just come in for a chat about the results of her latest cholesterol test and he can handle that. Is there something you wanted me to do instead?' This kind of phone call from Rosie rarely came without an ulterior motive.

'Mrs Wheeler's here. She doesn't have an appointment but she's in a bit of a state. I can't get the full story out of her, but something's happened with her daughter.' Rosie repeated Mrs Wheeler's patient number, knowing that looking her medical record up on the computer would be the first thing that Hope would do.

'Okay. Send Mrs Patel through to Theo. Could you tell him, please, that the only thing I wanted to see her for was the blood test. There are no other concerns. I'll come down to the waiting room to collect Mrs Wheeler. Thanks, Rosie.'

Hope scanned the screen quickly. She hadn't seen Joanne Wheeler for a while, and there were no outstanding issues, no clues about what had prompted today's visit. She made her way downstairs, and found Joanne sitting in the corner of the empty waiting room wiping her eyes with a handkerchief.

'Hello, Joanne.' Hope sat down next to her.

'I'm so sorry…'

'That's okay, you obviously need help with something. Before we do anything else, I need to ask you what's happening right now. Is there an emergency that we need to address? Something to do with your daughter, maybe?'

Joanne shook her head. 'No, Doctor. Amy's all right, although she's in hospital at the moment…' She dissolved into tears again.

'I'm sorry to hear that. Let's go upstairs and talk about why you're here, then.'

Hope waited while Joanne gathered her coat and handbag, nodding as Rosie quietly suggested that a cup of tea might be in order. By the time the receptionist arrived with it, Joanne was settled in a seat by Hope's desk, and seemed to be rallying.

'I shouldn't have come without an appointment.'

'That's okay. Just take a breath or two, and tell me what's bothering you.'

The story came spilling out. Joanne's seventeen-year-old daughter had gone to a party on Saturday evening, and been rushed to hospital in the early hours of Sunday morning, suffering from a drugs overdose. She was stable now, and the hospital would be sending her home the day after tomorrow.

'I don't know how to cope with it all…' Joanne turned the corners of her mouth down. 'My husband, Joel, and I… Joel said that we should search her room and we found three little bags of pills, hidden away.'

'I can see this is a really frightening situation for you. Can you do something for me, Joanne? I want you to take a breath.'

'I can't…'

'I know it's not easy. Just do your best.' Hope filled her own lungs with air, and Joanne followed suit. A few deep, steady breaths and she began to calm a little.

'That's good. Have you eaten today?'

Joanne shook her head. 'Neither of us can sleep, either.'

'When are you next going to see Amy?'

Joanne turned the corners of her mouth down. 'This evening. They're keeping her pretty busy during the day, with tests and talking sessions.'

'Those are the three things I want you to do this afternoon, then. Breathe, eat and sleep. And concentrate on doing all three of them as well as you can, cook a nice meal and sit down at the table to eat it. Make yourself a hot drink, close the curtains and just lie down for a little while. It's okay if you don't go to sleep, just try to get some rest. And if you feel yourself panicking, take a few breaths.'

Joanne frowned. 'That's not going to solve anything…'

'No, it isn't. But if you can keep your own strength up, then you'll be able to support Amy better. What's going on with your husband?'

'He's taken the week off work, as compassionate leave. This has just floored him. He wants to protect Amy but neither of us know how.'

'Okay, perhaps you can do what I said together, then.'

Joanne shook her head. 'But… We have to find someone for Amy. There's a drugs counsellor at the hospital and she's talked with him, but we don't know if that'll be enough.'

It was the start of what might be a long road. But Joanne was too fragile to hear that at the moment.

'Have you been able to speak to him? What's the situation with aftercare?'

'He says that there will be some, when she comes home. But I don't even know what she needs. This is all so new for us.'

'Leave it with me, just for this afternoon. There are a lot of different resources, and support's available for both Amy and for you, as her family. I'll be thinking about different options this afternoon, and come back to you with some choices that are available locally.' Hope knew that the hospital's drugs team would be following up on Amy's case, but ongoing care for the whole family was her responsibility. 'What time will you be going to see Amy this evening?'

'Six o'clock.'

'Then I'll call you at five, if that's okay.'

'Thank you, Doctor. I just don't know what to do for the best.'

'Right now, you need to take a few hours off. You can take this time to relax, knowing that I'll be doing some of the heavy lifting, eh?'

Hope recognised Joanne's sigh. She'd heaved that sigh herself a few times, when someone had told her to just stop and leave her mother's care to them for a while. 'Okay. We'll try.'

'Trying is good enough. What did you do with the pills you found, by the way?' Hope had set that question aside for the moment, but it was one that should be asked.

'We destroyed them.' Joanne pursed her lips. 'We could hardly put them back where they were, but Amy's going to realise we searched for them sooner or later. I'm not looking forward to that conversation.'

'I'll put that on the list of your immediate concerns. Leave it with me.'

Hope left the door of her consulting room ajar, waiting until she heard Theo bid Mrs Patel a cheery goodbye. Then she counted to ten, and made her way along the corridor. Breathless, again. In a good way, which seemed to lighten the load of the worries that patients left behind them.

'Can I ask a favour?'

He leaned back in his seat. 'If you want your pens back, I'm afraid I've already given one away.'

Of course he had. Hope had seen how Theo was with kids, and even as a young doctor he'd usually had something in his pocket to give a crying child. 'Nothing's changed, then.'

'Quite a lot's changed. Just not that.' A shadow seemed to form across his face, and then dispersed again as he smiled. 'What can I do for you?'

'I've just seen a lady who has a seventeen-year-old daughter in hospital—she's on the mend apparently, but she was rushed in over the weekend, after a drugs overdose.'

Theo nodded. 'And she turned up here, needing some help.'

'Yes. Maybe I should have taken Mrs Patel and left you to talk to her.'

He shrugged. 'You're the boss.'

No, not really, although she supposed she was senior to him now. Theo had never been her boss either, but he had known a great deal more than her when she was a third-year medical student, so she'd generally done whatever he'd told her to do. It seemed that they were still feeling their way in this new version of their relationship.

'I imagine you've dealt with a lot more situations like this than I have. And since I'm not in the habit of wasting what resources I have available...'

He grinned. 'I can speak to some of my contacts, and get a list of people in the area who'd be able to help. What are the specific concerns?'

'Just...a few ideas about where to start would be helpful. Although Joanne did mention to me that she and her husband had searched their daughter's room. She said that they found some pills, hidden away, and destroyed them. She knows she'll have to tell her daughter that they've been through all her belongings and that it's not going to be an easy conversation.'

Theo shook his head. 'No, it seldom is. Give me an hour and I'll put together a few thoughts on how to approach that.'

'Would you? You have time this afternoon?' Hope's satisfaction wasn't all on Amy's behalf. It was so good to be working with Theo again.

'I was thinking I might water my new plants, and then find out where the stationery cupboard is, but this sounds a lot more useful. Anything else to concentrate on…?'

Theo had always accepted that general practice was going to bring him into contact with patients with drug issues. No one had ever asked about the experience listed out on his CV, but Hope always asked when the welfare of a patient was at stake. And now he felt her guiding hand hovering over him, keeping him on track. He spent a busy afternoon, making calls to patients on the review list that Rosie had given him, and then completing his research on local resources for Joanne Wheeler and her husband.

Hope had set up a video call with Joanne and her husband, and invited Theo to join them. They spent nearly half an hour talking and Hope's support and reassurance, along with the information that Theo had compiled, had helped with that first, important step in the process of turning a teenager's life around.

'Thanks, Theo.' Hope leaned back in her seat, smiling. 'Your advice made all the difference. Joanne seems more confident that they can tackle this as a family now.'

'Sometimes all a teenager needs is a wake-up call and a supportive family.' Theo shrugged. He'd seen kids with everything going for them, who couldn't get themselves back onto the right road. Others who'd turned things around against all the odds.

'How do you deal with it? The uncertainty?'

'That's one of the reasons I don't do this kind of work full time any more.'

'What are you doing for dinner?' She was moving on now, with the practised ease of someone who knew she'd done her best and had to leave it at that. 'There's a nice eatery down by the seafront…?'

She left the invitation hanging. Casual and friendly, something that could be taken up, or turned down, with ease.

'I was thinking a takeaway, since I haven't got around to even switching the fridge in my flat on, let alone putting anything in it. But a little eatery down by the seafront sounds a much better option.'

A late spring breeze tugged at their jackets as they left the medical centre, becoming stronger as they reached the hotels and restaurants that lined the promenade. Hope turned into a doorway, leading him upstairs to a bright, busy seating area, and made a beeline for an empty table by the windows that faced the sea. Theo watched as she took off her coat, plumping herself down in a seat.

'You like looking out to sea?' He sat down opposite her.

'Yes. When I was little and we used to come down to the beach, I used to think of all the places that you could go, if you just put out to sea and sailed away. I lost sight of that over the years, when my mother became ill.'

'And now you see it again?' The open sky made Theo feel slightly weary, as if he'd already travelled into enough sunsets. 'Or is it too soon for that?'

'It's...' Hope spread her hands, shrugging. 'My mum's death wasn't unexpected. I'm still not quite sure what I want to do next, though. Everyone says *give it time*.'

'Sometimes things get to be clichés because they're true.'

She nodded, her eyes filling with tears. Hope brushed them away impatiently, as if they were something to be ashamed of. 'Sorry...'

'Don't be.'

'There's a lot to do... It's a big house.' Hope seemed keen to explain what didn't need to be explained to anyone. Theo leaned back in his chair, waiting for her to say whatever it was she wanted to say, and she smiled suddenly.

'Are you making me into a therapy project?'

Never. Hope wasn't a problem to be solved. Right now she seemed like the ultimate solution. The sunshine she carried with her, the sense of belonging... It all felt as if he'd found the home he craved.

'Force of habit.' He allowed himself to meet her

green-eyed gaze with a smile. 'Whatever you do, don't talk about it. I won't be listening.'

That made her laugh out loud. She picked up the menu that lay in front of her, glancing up at him every now and then as she studied it carefully. Theo laughed and did the same, covertly surveying her from behind his menu. By the time the waitress arrived to take their order, they were chuckling together, catching each other out, like a pair of incompetent private eyes.

Hope chose ravioli with a side salad, and Theo was hungry and went for a large portion of lasagne. He suggested a half-bottle of house red, and Hope nodded. Old friends, who didn't need to negotiate too much over their likes and dislikes,

Only they weren't. Theo hadn't known Hope for eighteen years, he'd known her eighteen years ago, and there was a difference. If he felt at home with her, then that was all an illusion, which he had to step away from. He was beginning to see that Hope was working through the process of spreading her wings, while his own mission in life was to find a place where he could settle.

'Where are you staying?' she asked.

'I've got a small flat, on the edge of town. A bed, a shower and an empty fridge. That's enough for me for the time being.'

'Until you find somewhere to call home?' Hope had always had a talent for the unspoken.

'Yeah. I reckon somewhere within easy reach

of London as it'll be easier to find a permanent job there. Close to Willow, but not too close. A place she knows she can come back to, whenever she wants.'

'And where *you* can put down a few roots?'

'I'd like that. I still want to make a difference, but I want a life that isn't governed by work, as well.'

Hope nodded. 'The elusive work-life balance. Let me know when you find it.'

Didn't she have that already? She appeared to, but then Hope was still making the journey towards living without her mother. Coming to terms with the fact that everything might change if she wanted it to, and deciding what she wanted to change.

'What happens if Willow decides to move away, after she's graduated?'

Theo chuckled. 'There are buses. Trains. Planes… It's about having a place, not where that place is.'

'And…someone?'

Theo had wondered about that, and realised that it wasn't too late to satisfy the obscure longing for someone to share his life with and that things didn't inevitably work out the way they had with Carrie. Now that he was settled he wouldn't face the same problems that had always put a time limit on his relationships. But he didn't want to talk about it with Hope, because right now it felt as if *she* was all he needed.

'I can handle Willow having boyfriends.' He deliberately misinterpreted the question. 'Just as long as they submit to a full blood work-up, a credit check and an enhanced DBS check. Along with in-depth counselling, to sort out any baggage they might be hauling around.'

Hope's outraged laughter was just as he expected. 'So you're a dad who worries, are you?'

'Of course. I try not to behave like one, though.'

'And what about her? Does she return the favour?'

Hope must know that it was an obvious question. A child who'd been abandoned in her teens would be forgiven for being a little possessive of the only carer she had left.

'Willow takes a keen interest in my love-life. I only need to spend ten minutes chatting to a single woman, outside work, and she's dropping hints about my giving her a call.'

Hope winced. 'Do I have to worry?'

Not about Willow. Maybe a little about Theo, but he was keeping those thoughts under wraps, at least until he knew more about the things that Hope very pointedly *hadn't* said.

'Nah. I won't tell her if you don't…' His phone rang and he took it from his pocket, a guilty grin spreading across his face. 'Hi, Willow… Yeah, everything's good… I'm with one of the other doctors at the practice at the moment, can I call you back later? Yeah, thanks for calling. I appreciate it.'

Theo stared at his phone for a moment, and then decided to put it back into his pocket. 'I don't *think* she's installed a tracker on my phone.'

'Would you know if she did?' Hope teased him.

'No, I don't have a clue about how these things work. Let's put it down to coincidence, she must have reckoned I'd be home by now and called to ask how my first day was.'

Hope nodded. 'Okay, we'll go with that. It would be awkward if you felt you had to throw your phone into the sea…'

It had been a great evening. A really good day, too. They'd walked back to the car park at the medical centre, and she'd watched as Theo had driven away.

Hope had thought about Theo so much during the last eighteen years. Woven a perfect life around the handsome, talented young man, which her own achievements couldn't possibly measure up to.

He hadn't changed so much. He still had that easy charm, and his eyes still held the promise that whatever the future held it would be a challenge to embrace. And now was really no different from when she'd first known him, Hope wasn't sure what her own future would be, but she knew it wouldn't be all about putting down roots. She had enough of those already, and was trying to disentangle herself from them.

Which was why she wasn't going to think about

the look in his eyes, or his smile. Wanting Theo was too hard to bear, because if she allowed him too close she ran the risk of disappointing him, just as she'd disappointed herself.

It was only a ten-minute drive home, and Hope got out of her car, surveying the large family house that was now hers. It looked good from the outside, with fresh paint, neatly trimmed bushes and spring flowers already in bloom. The shutters at the up-stairs windows allowed in the light, but protected the rooms from anyone's prying gaze.

She usually went around to the back, entering the house through the kitchen door where the stairs weren't right in front of her, seeming to mock her. But this time she walked to the front door, slid-ing her key into the lock. It was a little stiff, from lack of use, but the door swung open to reveal the long hallway.

There was one door to the right, which led to a light, airy sitting room, and another to the left, which she'd helped her mother turn into a bedroom after her father died. Further back, a smaller fam-ily room that Hope had been using as a bedroom ever since she'd moved in here, a bathroom and a large kitchen diner, which looked out over the back garden.

This had been Hope's domain, a clean, tidy and above all rubbish-free zone. Upstairs were stacks of old furniture and boxes, which made the rooms unliveable, but which her mother had guarded fiercely. She'd cry, and then linger in the hallway for days, to make sure that nothing else was taken away, if Hope tried to remove as much as a carrier bag. The two, completely different, floors of the house had been an uneasy solution, but the only one that had allowed Hope to ensure her mother's safety without breaking her heart.

Four months ago, Hope had inherited her parents' hoard of belongings, the boxes of newspapers, old clothes that were no longer wearable, every toy she'd played with as a child... Three old gramophones that her father had picked up at junk shops and brought home meaning to mend them and polish them up, but which still stood silent, crammed in with everything else.

She'd set out with good intentions, and made a start on emptying a few of the boxes, but she'd found herself in tears, putting everything back exactly where it had come from. All the things that her parents had saved so carefully over the years had grown in importance now she'd lost her mother. And she was caught now, pinned down by the weight of the hoard. Keeping it a secret, and never asking anyone back to the house, in case they climbed the stairs and saw what she was most ashamed of.

Hope ventured halfway up the stairs, wondering if this evening she might see the hoard in a different light—something that she *could* deal with. Then she chickened out, making a dash for the kitchen to make a cup of tea. It was no use. Theo couldn't come here and see this. Outside, in the sunshine, they could be friends, but she could never risk asking him back to see her home.

CHAPTER THREE

THEO HAD SPENT the week settling into the busy medical centre, finding his way around and learning how everyone liked to do things. Even his temporary assignment here, filling in during Dr Singh's maternity leave, was different because when that was over he didn't face moving again. He was a free agent, who could find another job in the area and stay as long as he wanted.

And it was good to have a friend, someone who'd known him for longer than six months. He had to be careful not to take up too much of Hope's time, because she had her own issues to deal with. She never spoke about her mother, but her silences, the abrupt changes in direction of a conversation, told him that her grief was still fresh.

'I spoke with Sara Jamieson about Amy and her family.' Hope bowled into his consulting room, still full of energy after a very full week's work.

'Yeah? How are they doing?' Theo had deliberately stepped back a little, reckoning that he'd done as much as he could to set everyone on the right track. The family were Hope's patients, and he knew she'd find him if she wanted to discuss anything.

'They're...' Hope shrugged. 'Amy's home, and physically she's recovering well. On an emotional level, Joanne tells me that some days are better than others.'

Theo nodded. 'Just having some better days is something to build on.'

'Yes, that's what I told her. She's joined one of the groups on your list, for parents of kids with drug problems. Amy didn't like that very much. Joanne went once and she made such a fuss that she hasn't gone again.'

'Doesn't like being a problem who gets talked about behind her back?' Theo suggested.

'Yes, that's pretty much it. Sara and I were wondering whether you might like to take the family on as your patients, since you have particular expertise that might help them.'

It sounded like an obvious move, but Theo hesitated. 'I'm a GP now. And I'm committed to that change.'

'Understood. But this is all part of a GP's work, isn't it?'

'I don't know the family as well as you do.'

'What's your *real* reason?' Hope was clearly not in the mood for excuses. He'd only ever spoken to one person about this, not family or friends, just his therapist. But he could give Hope the bare facts and leave out the part about his own life crashing and burning in response to one too many young lives lost to drugs.

'Coming home to England and becoming a GP wasn't one move, it was two. Willow had a place at university and I told the drugs agency I was working with that I needed to be here for her. They understood that—everyone gets to the point where travelling loses its charm—and I started work in London.'

'Doing the same kind of work that you'd been doing abroad?'

'Largely, yes. There was less emphasis on setting up brand-new facilities, and a little more on casework. An old friend contacted me. His son had become involved with drugs, and they'd been trying for years to help him. Several stints in rehab had failed and nothing seemed to be working. I said I'd do my best, and I got too involved.'

Hope's face darkened. She seemed to know what was coming but said nothing.

'Jonas was an amazing young man, had everything going for him. I'd seen cases like his before but this time... When he died from a drugs overdose, I knew that I needed to go back into general practice, to regain some balance.'

'I'm so sorry, Theo. I shouldn't have asked you about Amy, without knowing the full story.'

'It's okay... I'd just rather not be too closely involved. Maybe I could help out, rather than take Amy on as a patient?' It was a risk, but one that Theo felt able to take. He'd put some distance between himself and what had happened with Jonas, and done some healing. And this time he had Hope on his side.

She hesitated for a moment, clearly not completely buying into the idea that Theo's decision had been as easy as he made it sound. 'So I'll keep Joanne and her family on my list, but you might be able to give some input now and again. Are you sure that's okay, Theo?'

'It's fine. If I get too involved, you'll drag me away into a corner and give me a talking-to?'

Hope laughed, giving him a nod. There had been times when Theo had done the same—explaining the limitations and what they could and couldn't do for their patients. And times when he'd held her, when she'd cried over a particularly challenging patient. That seemed far more special now than it had then.

'I'll be glad to return the favour. I've promised to pop in early this evening. Would you like to come? You don't need to pretend you're busy if you don't want to, a *no* will do.' She shot him an impish look.

Theo chuckled. 'In that case, it'll be a *yes*. Thanks.'

The family lived on the outskirts of Hastings, half an hour's drive away. Hope had decided to keep things brief for starters, and just introduce herself and Theo to Amy, and let her know that they were both there to listen and answer her questions. Theo seemed relaxed and rather less worried about the meeting than she was.

'How did I do?' Hope asked as she settled herself back in the driving seat of her car.

'Fine. Great, actually. You didn't come across as judging Amy, and you made it clear that we were there for her. You ran through the options available to her, and emphasised that what she wanted was important to you.'

Hope puffed out a breath. 'She didn't seem terribly interested in any of them.'

'Well, she's been through a lot in the last week, both physically and mentally. I suspect that her one aim in life at the moment is for everyone to leave her alone. Let her think about it a bit, and we'll see if she comes to any conclusions.'

'Thanks, Theo. I really do appreciate your help.'

He nodded an acknowledgement. 'Do you fancy a coffee? My place is on your way home, and I have an ulterior motive.'

'You do?' Hope would bet her last shilling that Theo's ulterior motive was entirely honourable, and bit back her disappointment. 'In that case, you'd better give me directions.'

The flat was on the top floor of a small block, set back from the road slightly. Neat and utilitarian, it was the kind of building that would be easy to walk past without even noticing it was there.

'It's a bit… I haven't got around to many home comforts yet. I do however have milk and coffee…' Theo let her walk ahead of him into the sitting room, clearly expecting that Hope wouldn't much like the place.

But she did. Cream walls, wooden blinds at the window, and a timber floor. Not a great deal of furniture, there was a sofa, a TV and not much else, but that made Hope feel somehow lighter.

'I like it. It's uncluttered.'

Theo looked around. 'Yes, I suppose that's one thing it has going for it.'

'Don't knock it, Theo. I have a bit of decluttering to do at home.' Decluttering sounded rather more everyday and civilised than…whatever it was that needed doing to her place. That probably involved a lot of heavy lifting, both mentally and physically.

He chuckled, walking through the open archway that led to the kitchen. White kitchen units, with a wooden counter top, which was completely clear, apart from a coffee machine. 'You brought that with you?'

'Yeah. How did you guess?'

It wasn't white, for starters. And it was a little more complex than the kind of kitchen equipment rental properties usually provided. What would it be like to just leave everything behind, and come and live in a place like this? Somewhere that faded into the background, and wasn't constantly tearing at her.

'So what's your ulterior motive? Do I need coffee first?'

'Yeah. Maybe.' Theo took two mugs from a half-empty cupboard and set about making the coffee.

'You're planning on staying here?'

'In the short term. It's a bit basic, but it suits me at the moment. I guess if I'd brought a bit more than a carload of things with me, it might be a bit more welcoming.'

'Surely you have furniture, though. Is that in storage?'

Theo shook his head. 'When I was abroad, the agency used to deal with accommodation. We stayed in some really nice places, and they were all fully furnished. It's not really practical to have furniture when you're moving around so much. When I was in London I rented a furnished flat and when I came here I had to organise this place in a hurry, so I took what I could get.'

'Well, this is great, Theo. You can really make it yours, and if you move on and buy a place then you'll have some bits and pieces to make a start with. You said you wanted somewhere that you could call home, didn't you?'

'Yes, I did say that, didn't I?' Theo frowned, and suddenly the penny dropped.

'That's the ulterior motive, isn't it?'

He nodded. 'Not so much here...' He beckoned for Hope to follow him, and walked out into the hallway, leading her past the open door of a bedroom, which contained a bed and a wardrobe.

Opening a door further down the hall, he stood back so that Hope could enter first.

'This is nice, too. It's really light in here.' Hope looked around. In addition to the bed and wardrobe, there was a large old-fashioned leather trunk in the corner of the room. 'Is that yours?'

'It's Willow's. After her mother left, the thing she needed most was security and continuity, and one of the things I did was to get her this. Having her own things around her made her feel safe and I told her that she could put whatever she wanted in it, and that it would always travel with us and be in her room wherever she went. She doesn't have room for it in her student digs, so it's here.'

'This is Willow's room?'

'Yeah. She'll always have her own room, wherever I go. That was part of the bargain as well.'

'It's a beautiful thing. I bet you can get quite a lot into it.'

Suddenly, clutter took on a whole new meaning. It held memories, kept them safe from the passage of time and the pain of loss. Maybe Hope should think about her own problem that way, although the difference in scale made the hoard confronting rather than comforting.

If full spaces were a challenge, then she could tackle empty ones. Hope looked around the room. 'So you want to make this nice for Willow?'

He nodded. 'She loves colour and light. Remember the room you had when you shared a house?'

She remembered. Hope hadn't been there long, but she'd loved that room. It was still the only place she'd lived that felt truly hers.

'That had cream-coloured walls, as well.'

Theo chuckled. 'Yeah, and you filled it with colour. Willow's taste is a lot like yours and I was wondering if you had a spare afternoon to come shopping with me. There's no particular rush. She won't be coming to stay here until the end of term.'

'Won't she want to choose her own things?'

'Oh, she adds to whatever I do. But I want to show her that I've made an effort, at least. And a bit more furniture wouldn't go amiss. Somewhere to put her shoes—she has lots of them.'

'You mean more than two pairs? That's a very positive thing, Theo.'

'See. You *do* have a much better handle on this than I do.'

'I'm beginning to think so. Let me have a think over the weekend, and I'll come up with some ideas. You need to have ideas first, before you commit to anything.'

'Right you are.' Theo beamed at her. 'I don't suppose you fancy a pizza, do you? There's a nice place, around the corner from here…'

Theo had been missing Hope fiercely, all weekend. Looking around his flat, seeing it through her eyes. Even dreaming of her, when sleep robbed him of the discipline to prevent himself from wondering what it might be like to be more than a friend to her. On Monday morning, after a full list of patients, he was catching up with his notes and wondering what to have for lunch when Hope walked into his consulting room, carrying a box. She laid it on his desk with something that looked like triumph in her green eyes and, caught unawares, he found himself melting in the heat of her gaze.

'What's this? A kitchen blender?' It was an effort to look away from her smile and focus on the box.

'No, that's just the box. It's something for Willow.'

That was nice of her. Theo got to his feet, peeling back the packing tape and taking out the bubble-wrapped package inside.

'This is lovely. Don't you want to keep it, Hope?' A blue and green dragonfly-design Tiffany-style lamp had emerged from the wrappings. The shade was fringed with iridescent beads, which caught the light, and the brass stand gleamed softly.

From her no-nonsense glare, he'd clearly said the wrong thing. 'I have a pair that I like much better in my sitting room. This one's been wrapped up in storage for years, and there's no point in it if it never sees the sun, is there?'

'I suppose not but—are you sure?' Theo couldn't help asking, even if his question clearly didn't conform to whatever plan Hope had.

'Positive. Some of the beads have come off, but

they were saved.' She reached into the box and drew out an envelope. 'And there's an electrical place in the old town, which will test it for safety and change the fitting so that you can use it with an LED bulb.'

It was time to give in and accept the gift gracefully. 'Thank you. Willow will love it.'

Hope gave him a luminous smile. 'It's my pleasure. I hope it's a nice welcome for her.'

'It will be. I'll take it down to get it fixed and tested at the weekend, and leave the beads for her to reattach. She's good with her hands, she'll make a better job of it than me, and she likes making things.'

'It'll look as good as new, then.' Hope was looking at the lamp with obvious satisfaction.

'It'll be better than new. It's a lovely gift.' And the best gift of all was her smile. For some reason this meant something to her, something more than just the perfect decoration for a bland and uninspiring room. It meant more to Theo as well, because it was important to Hope.

'Can I buy you lunch?' Maybe Hope would give him a clue about why this gesture seemed of such consequence. 'Or dinner?'

'Absolutely, but I have to take a rain check for today, I'm really busy. I'm glad you think Willow will like it...' Hope turned on her heel, hurrying out of the room almost abruptly, leaving Theo to wonder what had just happened here.

He sat down, running his finger through the hanging beads that fringed the glass shade. Hope might appear enigmatic at times, but he'd learned that there was always a method, always some plan behind everything she did. If he waited, then perhaps she'd share it with him.

CHAPTER FOUR

PRIDE CAME BEFORE a fall...

Hope had done some serious thinking over the weekend. And Theo had given her the jolt she'd needed to go and investigate the contents of some of the crates that were stacked in the front bedroom. After several hours of searching she'd found the Tiffany-style lamp that almost matched the two in the sitting room, but not quite, and then there had been the added excitement of sorting through the stack of flattened cardboard boxes, to find one that was the right size.

'There you go, Dad. You said they'd come in handy at some point, didn't you?'

She'd murmured the words, hoping that no more justification was needed to put the treasure she'd found on the back seat of her car, ready to take into the medical centre on Monday morning.

And she *was* proud of herself. She'd found a home for something she'd never use, and, even if it made no discernible difference to the collection of things that filled the room, it was a first step in the right direction. And Theo had clearly liked her gift. She'd escaped back to her own consulting room before she'd been tempted to hug him.

They'd been busy that week, and lunch would have to wait. Theo had unexpectedly said that he'd go and see Amy and her family on Thursday evening, and Hope hadn't argued. He'd seemed confident about going alone, and she'd had another plan forming in her head.

Hope sat down for half an hour with her customary after-work cup of tea and then set to work. She changed into a pair of comfortable sweatpants and pulled the loft steps down from the ceiling. The loft was boarded out and well-lit and it was easy to find the three matching side tables that she had in mind. They were plain and simple, of good quality, and they'd do for both Willow's bedroom and the sitting room. She'd take one of them downstairs, clean it up and show Theo a photograph tomorrow. Hope manoeuvred the table carefully out of the loft and as she carried it downstairs, she wondered whether delivering the tables might be a good excuse to go and see Theo at the weekend...

And then she came back down to earth with a bump.

Breathe for a moment, or at least try to. Take it slow. Don't panic. That was all good advice, but all Hope could hear were her own whimpering cries. The shock of falling halfway down the stairs had scattered her senses, and then the table had landed on top of her and sent agonising pain shooting up her left leg.

'Don't cry...' That was too late, she was already crying. 'ABC.' The protocol for dealing with an injured patient didn't help either. Hope knew her

Airways were clear and that she was Breathing, and couldn't feel any signs of major blood loss that might compromise her Circulation. All she could feel was the pain in her leg.

'Get help.' That was easier said than done. She'd taken her phone with her when she'd gone up into the loft, but it must have slipped out of her pocket as she fell, because it wasn't there now.

First things first. Her head swam as she sat up, and just removing the broken pieces of the table from her legs really hurt. Her left ankle was already swelling, and a little gentle probing with her fingers told her that although it was showing all the signs of being fractured, the fracture wasn't displaced. That was good news.

Only to a point. Hope was feeling a little light-headed, and just touching the cool quarry tiles beneath her made her feel queasy. The emotional shock of the fall was beginning to set in, and she had to call someone.

'Phone...' She looked around and saw her phone lying on the floor, within reach. By some miracle it was still working, and before she'd had a chance to think, she found herself texting Theo. He wouldn't be answering his phone if he was still with Amy and her family, but he was the only person she wanted to call. The only one she could call.

Please call me.

That sounded a little too urgent.

When you have a chance.

She sent the text and then reconsidered, wondering if that didn't sound urgent enough. She was typing a second text when her phone rang.

'Theo!' Tears of relief started to run down her face.

'What's up?' The tension in his voice told her that he already knew something was wrong.

'I fell.'

'I'm in the car now. Give me your address, Hope.'

The question didn't register. 'I think…my ankle may be broken…'

'Hope. Listen to me. Give me your postcode, for the satnav.' His tone was calm, suddenly, reassuring. Of course. The first thing he needed to know was where she was. Hope gave him her postcode and then her house number. That would be enough for him to find her.

'Wait a moment while I get the directions. Stay on the line, Hope.'

She heard the synthetic voice of the satnav repeating back her full address, and that prompted more tears. 'That's right…'

'Okay, I'll be ten minutes. What's the best way for me to get into the house?'

'Back door. Walk round to the back door.' Force

of habit lent certainty to her words. He mustn't see…

'Got it. Back door. I want you to stay where you are. Wait for me to get there.'

No chance. Hope was beginning to feel a little better now, if she ignored the pain in her ankle. It was one thing for Theo to come to the house, and quite another to have him walking through the hallway, where he might find a reason to go upstairs.

'I'm okay, Theo. I don't need you to stay on the line. Just concentrate on the road and I'll see you in ten minutes.'

She heard him chuckle. Clearly the application of two slightly longer sentences had reassured him. 'Sure you don't want to answer a few easy questions?'

'No, Theo. I'm fully conscious, breathing without any difficulty, and responsive.' Somehow it was a little easier to remember basic medical checks, than it was to think about the complexities of this particular situation.

'Fair enough. Stay put and I'll be there soon.'

As soon as she'd ended the call, Hope ignored Theo's perfectly reasonable advice. Sliding across the quarry tiles in the hall was painful but easy enough, and she couldn't fall any further than this. The wooden floors of the seating space to one side of the kitchen were no problem either, and Hope could reach up and flip the latch on the door.

'Almost done…' She muttered the words, holding her left leg clear of the floor as she slid carefully towards the sofa. Then she could reach for one of the cushions, place it under her ankle, and relax.

Theo looked around as he opened the glazed back door. There was a large kitchen area to one side of the wide space, with a table and chairs in the middle. Further along, by a brick fireplace, two sofas. Then he saw Hope, sitting on the floor in front of one of the sofas, her leg propped on a cushion.

Leaving the door on the latch, in case he needed to go back out to his car, Theo applied a smile to his face. He could see no evidence of Hope having fallen in here, but decided to leave that particular question, in favour of a few more medically relevant ones.

'Heard you could do with a doctor.'

'A friend…' That answered one question, at least. 'Although I could do with a doctor, as well.'

Theo nodded, kneeling down beside her. 'May I take a look?'

Hope nodded, a trace of reluctance in her face. The leg of her sweatpants was pulled up, and he could see that her ankle was already red and swollen. She twisted her face as he gently probed it, deciding that Hope had self-diagnosed correctly and she was going to need an X-ray. But her pallor and the telltale shakiness that accompanied a bad fall were worrying him a little more at the moment.

'Looks like you took quite a tumble. Did you bang your head?'

'I don't think so.'

Theo took that as an invitation to check for any lumps or contusions and found nothing. Then he clipped a pulse oximeter from his medical bag to her finger, and took her blood pressure, checking her breathing for good measure.

'Not bad.'

That prompted the response he wanted, and Theo saw a spark of outrage animate her face. 'Not bad? What do you mean, not bad?'

He grinned. 'Pretty good, actually, considering the circumstances. May I take a look at your other leg?'

Hope pressed her lips together, allowing him to roll the leg of her sweatpants up. She had a graze on her knee, and more red marks that would be turning into bruises over the next day or so. She'd fallen from a height.

'Okay. This didn't happen in here, did it?'

The look on her face told him that his suspicions were correct. 'I was carrying something down the stairs and I lost my balance...' A tear rolled down her cheek.

All he wanted to do was to comfort her, but Theo needed to know. He got to his feet, pushing the kitchen door open and looking down the hall. There was a mess of wood at the bottom of the stairs that looked like the remnants of a coffee table, and when he saw the patterned quarry tiles of the floor, and thought of her crashing down onto them, it was an almost physical shock.

He turned, closing the door behind him, and made his way quickly back to her. Hope was trying to wipe her face with the sleeve of her sweat top, and Theo did the one and only thing possible. He took her gently into his arms.

She flinched a little as she stretched up to hug him, but that didn't stop her from hanging on tight. Theo felt her heart racing, or maybe it was his.

'I've got you. It's going to be all right.'

'I'm so sorry, Theo. Bringing you all this way...'

'This is exactly where I want to be. Never doubt that, Hope.' Right now, he was no doctor. He was someone who wanted to dry her tears and comfort her. A man who wanted to hold her and keep her safe.

But this wasn't the practical help that Hope needed. He had to assess her injuries. He held her close for a few moments longer and then gently disengaged her arms from around his neck, resisting the temptation to leave just one fleeting kiss on her cheek.

'You're going to need an X-ray on your ankle, and someone should take a look at those bruises as well.'

She nodded, twisting her lips in an expression

of regret that made his heart jump wildly. It *hadn't* been just a hug of reassurance, which could be left behind without a second thought. Theo ignored the feeling that something special had been found and then lost again, and pressed on.

'Before we go anywhere I have to check there's nothing more...' Hope knew exactly what he meant. It was unlikely that there was anything more than bruising to her ribs and hips, Hope had obviously contrived to get from the bottom of the stairs to here, but Theo had to make sure.

He unzipped her sweatshirt, pulling up the sleeves of the T-shirt underneath. She had an angry red blotch on one shoulder and he reckoned that there were probably bruises forming on her hip, as well.

Then the hard part. Theo applied all of his con-centration to looking for signs of injury to her ribs and hips, his fingers checking for anything un-toward, his gaze on her face for any signs of pain. Once that was accomplished, he turned to the less challenging task of applying a flexible splint to her ankle and bandaging it.

'Got any ice packs? We'll probably have to wait a while, in A & E.' He sat back on his heels, and Hope nodded.

'In the fridge. There are tea towels in the drawer next to the sink.'

'And they say doctors make the worst patients.' He chuckled as he opened the large fridge-freezer, and then reconsidered as he turned and saw Hope easing herself carefully up onto the sofa. 'Hey! What do you think you're doing?'

'Now you've splinted my ankle, I think I can make it around to the car...' Hope was gripping the arm of the sofa, clearly trying to struggle to her feet.

It wasn't so much a matter of losing his head, more a case of finding out what he was really here for. He strode to the sofa, sitting down next to her. 'Hold on to me, Hope. I've got this.'

Her eyes widened suddenly, and then she put her arm around his shoulders, clutching at his shirt. This *was* what he was here for, to be strong when she was hurt and vulnerable.

'Thank you...' She nestled against him as Theo lifted her up in his arms, and carefully carried her out to the car.

The A & E department of the local hospital wasn't too busy, and they were in and back out again within two hours. Theo had been as solid as a rock. Strong, steady and yet almost unbearably tender. He'd lifted her up effortlessly, and she'd clung to him as he'd carried her to the car, feeling his warmth and the swell of muscle beneath her fingertips.

This wasn't Hope's imagination and it wasn't the instinct to cling to someone who'd come to the rescue when you were hurt. It was something more, but Hope couldn't think about that. She'd let Theo inside her house because she'd had to, and managed to avoid allowing him to see upstairs. That could only last for so long. And his presence here in Hastings wasn't permanent either, it was probably only until Anna Singh returned from maternity leave. Even if he could accept her most embarrassing secrets, he'd be moving on.

It was dark by the time they got back, but the security lights flipped on as they walked back around the house to the kitchen door. Hope wasn't used to the two elbow crutches and the orthopaedic boot, which reached almost up to her knee, but Theo let her struggle a little, there to catch her if she fell but allowing her to find the best way of doing things on her own.

She breathed a sigh of relief as he closed the kitchen door behind them. 'Thank you so much, Theo. I don't know what I would have done without you.'

'I'm glad I was here.' He shot her a querying look. Maybe he saw the oddness of it all, the big, empty house, no one but him to call when she was in trouble. But he said nothing.

'You should be going. You have work tomorrow.'

'That's okay. It's too early to go to bed and I've nothing else to do. Why don't you sit down and I'll make you a drink?'

Hope hesitated. The doors were all locked upstairs, and she'd retracted the loft steps before bringing the table down. If he did stray up there, she could just tell him the same as she'd told her mother's carers—that the first floor of the house was closed up. She hadn't really needed to crawl in here, earlier, but she'd panicked at the thought of Theo coming to the house.

And she wanted him to stay. She could tell him not to make a fuss of her, but that was what she really wanted Theo to do. She could take a risk for the reward of having him close a little longer.

'I don't suppose… Would you mind just sticking around while I take a hot shower? The bathroom's right next door and I had grab rails and a shower seat installed for Mum.'

He nodded. 'I'll collect up that broken furniture from the bottom of the stairs, shall I?'

Hope swallowed hard. 'Thanks. But don't take it back upstairs. Leave it outside, by the back door, and I'll have it taken away…' She supposed that was one way of decreasing the collection of furniture, but having to throw herself down the stairs made it a one-time-only solution.

'Sure.' He shot her another of those querying looks. 'Are you okay?'

Hope straightened herself, smiling. 'Yes, I'm fine. I'll be better when I've had a shower and changed out of these clothes.'

'All right. Call if you need me.'

She didn't need him, and she didn't call. Hope

showered, and changed into her most sensible nightdress and dressing gown, finding that the hall had been cleared and swept when she emerged from the bathroom. Theo was in the kitchen, making hot chocolate.

'Better?' He turned, smiling.

'Much.' Hope was suddenly very tired, hiding a yawn behind her hand.

'You want to go and lie down? I'll bring your drink in to you.'

Lying on her bed was so far down on her list of embarrassments about her home that it didn't even feature. Hope made her way slowly into her bedroom, and Theo followed, propping pillows behind her back and under her legs and handing her a couple of painkillers with hot chocolate to wash them down.

'Ah… Thank you, Theo. That's so much more comfortable.' Hope was beginning to feel really drowsy now, but she wanted him to stay. 'How did things go with Amy this evening? Is she okay?'

He took the hint, sitting down in the armchair by the window. 'It was good. Amy's coming to terms with the idea that her parents need some support with this as well, and isn't giving Joanne such a hard time about going to a group herself. We talked a bit about saying how you felt without making it sound like an accusation.'

Hope nodded. '*I feel this* instead of *You did that*.'

'Yeah. I had to help with a bit of rewording, for

starters, but it turned into a really constructive conversation.'

'Is she sleeping any better?'

Theo shook his head. 'No, and that's not helping. I'm loth to prescribe medication though, and so I made a few suggestions about a more natural approach. Joanne said she'd try those out too, and Amy seemed to like the idea.'

'Sounds good. Even if it doesn't work, they'll be doing something together to care for each other. It sounds as if Amy's beginning to see that it's not her against the world.' Hope stifled a yawn, trying to keep her eyes open, and the next thing she knew Theo was gently removing the cup of hot chocolate from her grasp.

'I think we won't add scalds to bruising and a broken bone, if that's okay with you.'

'Anything you say, Theo…'

'Really?' She heard him laugh. 'You're starting to worry me, now.'

She chuckled drowsily. She was warm and comfortable, and no longer frightened and wondering how badly she'd hurt herself. Theo had made everything right.

Hope must have dozed off, because when she opened her eyes she could hear Theo moving around in the kitchen. She went to sit up, and groaned as pain shot through her shoulder and hip.

Theo appeared in the doorway of the bedroom, a plate of toast in one hand and a mug in the other.

'You should be getting home. It must be late. Why are you making toast, Theo?'

'It's seven o'clock. You've been asleep for nearly nine hours.'

'Ah. That explains why I'm aching so badly.' Hope sat up gingerly. 'And feeling so awake.'

'Yeah, probably. Look, I need to get going in half an hour, to get home and changed before I start work. Is there anything you need?'

'Coffee…?' She looked at the mug he was carrying.

He put the mug down on the bedside table, and Hope caught the scent of a fresh brew. 'Anything else?'

'No. Thank you, Theo.' A thought occurred to her. 'You haven't been up all night, have you?'

'No, I crashed out on the sofa.' He grinned. 'Much more comfortable than that old sofa you used to have in your student digs.'

'That's not saying much. I'll be in a little late today—'

'No, you will not. You're not coming in to work at all.' He frowned at her.

'But it's Sara Jamieson's day off today. She's working this weekend. I'll be okay. I just need to take things slowly.'

'Yes, you do need to take things slowly, and no, you won't be okay coming into work. I'll get Rosie to organise some help from the practice nurse and the physician associate and between the three of us we'll manage.' Hope opened her mouth to argue and he silenced her with a glare. 'What happened to "Anything you say, Theo"? Have you forgotten about that?'

'I was half asleep. Clearly I was incoherent.'

He chuckled. 'Thought it was too good to be true. By the time you've got up, had a shower and iced your bruises it'll be lunchtime. I'll speak to you then.'

Maybe he was right. Maybe not. 'You don't happen to know where my painkillers are, do you?'

Theo clearly reckoned that was a tacit agreement. He grinned, disappearing for a moment and coming back with the box of tablets. 'See you later?'

'Thanks, Theo. Yes, I'll see you later.'

CHAPTER FIVE

THERE WAS A long list of patients for Theo to see this morning, but by one o'clock the pressure had eased. People seemed to be disappearing from his list, and Theo reckoned that Rosie must have set up an impromptu triage system, and was diverting patients who didn't need to see a doctor to Colette the nurse, or Amir, the physician associate. His phone rang, and Rosie instructed him that he now had half an hour for lunch. Theo decided not to enquire too closely into how she'd managed to engineer that, as half an hour was exactly what he needed right now.

He picked up his phone, dialling Hope's number. Her ringtone drifted through the open window and he frowned, getting to his feet and following the sound along the corridor. As he paused outside her consulting room, she answered.

'Hi, Theo.'

Her voice sounded bright and firm. Theo pushed open the door and saw her sitting behind her desk.

'How are you doing?' He walked into the room and sat down, trying not to frown. 'Resting up?'

She flushed guiltily and then shot him an annoyed look. 'All right. Clearly I was going to mention that I was here, at some point.'

'Of course. Because clearly I was going to notice.'

'Theo! Don't make a fuss about it. I was feeling okay and starting to get bored, so I called a taxi to bring me here. And you can't tell me you didn't need the help. I've seen four patients in the last hour.'

'And I expect your ankle's hurting...' Perhaps he should sound a little less annoyed. Patients generally didn't like it when their doctors were unsympathetic to their pain. Although Hope was neither a patient nor a doctor at the moment, she was a friend who he cared about.

'Not really. Throbs a bit.' She jutted her chin in his direction.

'If it's throbbing then you should be elevating it, not sitting behind a desk. And by the way, what's with texting me yesterday evening, instead of calling?'

'I knew you were with Amy and I didn't want to interrupt.'

'So you fell down the stairs, broke your ankle, and thought that wasn't important enough to call me. That's just perverse. Whatever I was doing could have waited.' What really hurt was that Hope wouldn't acknowledge how much she meant to him. She'd been his first priority last night, and she was his first priority now.

'Remember what you were saying about Amy and her family last night, Theo? About accusatory language?'

'Oh, so you *were* listening to something I had

to say.' That was unnecessary, as well as accusatory. Theo tried to reword, but his jumbled emotions wouldn't allow him to. 'I… It was a shock to find you here.'

Suddenly the angry fire in her eyes died. 'Look, I'm really busy at the moment, and so are you. Can't we talk about this later?'

Later. That was a very good suggestion. Theo nodded and got to his feet.

Hope had half expected him to slam the door behind him. At least that would have given her the opportunity to shout something about not coming back until he'd readjusted his attitude, in his wake. That would have let off a bit of steam, but in the long term it wouldn't have solved anything.

Theo was right to be angry with her. Coming in to work today had felt like a good idea, but she should have listened to him, because it wasn't. She'd leave him to cool down for a while and then go and apologise.

But he beat her to it. Fifteen minutes later, there was a tap on the door, and he entered, carrying a cup of coffee from the café across the street.

'I'm really sorry. I was upset that you were hurt, and angry with myself because I felt it was my fault. I shouldn't have blamed you for that.'

'You have nothing to apologise for, Theo. Why on earth would you think it was your fault?'

He shrugged. 'When I cleared up the mess at

the bottom of the stairs, it was difficult not to notice that it was a broken coffee table. Would it be presumptuous to assume that it had something to do with my empty sitting room?'

She hadn't realised… Hope supposed she could tell Theo that it was nothing to do with him, and that she'd had a sudden urge to move furniture around. But in this, at least, he deserved a bit of honesty.

'It was for you—if you wanted it. It's presumptuous to assume that it was your fault that I fell. That's entirely down to me. I'm not inclined to accept an apology for that.'

He put the cardboard beaker down on her desk and took a seat. Clearly that wasn't all Theo had on his mind.

'What else, Theo?'

'I just… I heard the alert for your text while I was driving and I was going to call you when I got home. Then I got stuck in traffic at the lights…' He shook his head. 'I can't help thinking that I nearly left you lying at the bottom of the stairs while I got home and made myself a cup of tea.'

'That was my decision too, Theo. If it's any consolation, I was typing another text to say it was urgent, when you rang.'

He smiled suddenly. 'Yeah. I would have answered that, even if I'd been clinging to a cliff face, over a pool of crocodiles.'

Hope chuckled. 'Easy to say in Hastings. We don't have much of a crocodile problem here.'

'Hanging by one finger, watching a crack open up above me, at Beachy Head?' That toe-tingling grin of his was making her ankle throb.

'Yes, I guess you could have been doing that.' There were questions that Theo still wasn't asking. The answers were embarrassing but he deserved to hear them and suddenly Hope wanted to close the gap that existed between them.

'To be honest, Theo... You're the only friend I could call. I don't want to presume on you always being there.'

He shot her a look of honest disbelief. Hope supposed it wasn't the most obvious of things to say. She'd lived in Hastings almost all her life and was surrounded by people.

'You had loads of friends at university...' he murmured.

'Yes, but that was different. When you're a carer you tend to keep people at arm's length, because you know that if they suggest doing something you'll end up either saying no, or cancelling at the last minute. I *do* have friends, really good ones, mostly other carers that I've met. We've supported each other for years, and we understand that a message on an Internet group is generally the most we can do.'

'And you needed someone who could come.' Understanding sparked in his eyes.

'Yes. I still keep up with the group, but in the evenings, no one can leave the person they're caring for alone. You were the only real friend that I could call, and maybe you don't know quite how much that means to me...' Hope was feeling a little breathless now. She'd practically admitted that Theo was becoming the centre of her world.

'I didn't realise.' His brow creased. 'That's what you're doing here now. You wanted people around you.'

'Does that sound stupid?'

'No.' Theo shook his head. 'Everyone loses their confidence a bit after a fall like that. I'm glad you called me, last night. I wouldn't have wanted to be anywhere else.'

He meant it. She could see from the warmth in his eyes that he *really* meant it. They were both finding their way in a new world and maybe they both needed this friendship a lot more than either was willing to admit.

Hope focussed on the mug on her desk. 'I don't suppose the coffee's for me, is it?'

'Yes, of course it is.'

'That's really nice of you. Thank you.' She peeled open the lid and caught her breath. 'Theo! Whipped cream and chocolate curls.'

'Can't go wrong with chocolate curls.' He pursed his lips. 'Would it be too pushy of me to ask whether you're intending seeing any more patients this afternoon? Rosie caught me on my way back in with the coffee, and I can handle all of the appointments myself.'

'My leg is beginning to hurt a bit. I have a few patient reviews to catch up on.' Maybe she should compromise and offer to go home and do that.

'I'm sure there's nothing that wouldn't wait until Monday.' Theo shot her a grin. 'But since you're here, you may as well be comfortable.'

He pulled the curtains back from around the couch in the corner of the room, and released the lever to lower it. Then he raised the backrest. It *did* look far more inviting than her chair felt at the moment. Hope got to her feet, and Theo waited while she grabbed her crutches and walked slowly towards him.

'Good idea.' She smiled up at him, and Theo nodded.

She sat down on the couch, swinging her legs up onto it. Theo leaned over to adjust the backrest a little, and put a pillow beneath her injured leg, and then fetched her laptop from her desk. Then he took the plants off a small side table by the window, and placed it next to her, with her coffee within reach.

'That's much better. Thanks, Theo.' His help was a little different now. Theo wasn't just someone who would care for her when she was hurt, he was a man who claimed the right to do so. And Hope had to admit that managing on her own lost its lustre when he was around. She could still feel the brush of his fingers, still smell his clean, warm scent.

She couldn't help gazing at him as he walked back towards her desk, seeing only the coiled strength in his body. Hope swallowed down the lump in her throat as he picked her phone up, then turned, smiling as he handed it to her.

'Call me if there's anything you need.'

'I will. You have your car here, today?'

'In the car park.' The amused look in his eyes told her that he wasn't going to offer, she would have to ask. She was going to have to meet him halfway, because that was what friends did.

'Would you give me a lift home? I'm comfortable here, and there's plenty I can be getting on with until you're ready to leave.'

His smile somehow managed to combine a hint of triumph with its warmth. 'My pleasure…'

As apology experiences went, that had been a good one. Willow had taught him that chocolate was capable of some heavy lifting when he needed to express remorse, and Hope had confirmed the theory. She was perfectly capable of making herself a bit more comfortable, but she'd let him help her. And the *way* she'd allowed it, making it seem like something she wanted as much as he did, had quietened his raging heart.

He was tempted to rush through the patients that remained on his list for this afternoon, but he knew better than that. Hope was able to access the network from her laptop, and he had little doubt that she'd be checking his notes on a few of the people who she'd been scheduled to see for follow-ups. Anything less than his usual meticulous notes wouldn't do, and so he listened carefully to Mr Constable's update on the situation with his garden fence, knowing that stress management was an integral part of his physical ailments. It was six o'clock before he bade his final patient a cheery goodbye, but the look on Hope's face when he tapped on the door and walked into her consulting room told him that she'd been more than happy to wait.

'How did it go with Mrs Abeila?' Hope clearly wasn't going to allow him to prioritise her own injury.

'Much happier with her new medication. It doesn't upset her stomach as much. I suggested that she might try taking it in the afternoon or evening, to see whether that improved things even more.'

'Mr Constable...?'

'Apparently his new neighbour is much more reasonable than the old one, and they've sorted out the boundary dispute amicably. I wouldn't like to say that's entirely responsible for his blood-pressure reading, but I expect it helped. Didn't you read my notes?'

Hope flushed slightly, and Theo felt an inexplicable urge to press his lips against her cheek. 'Sorry. I'm not checking up on you.'

'That's okay, check all you want. Just remember to save and close when you've finished reading something, because we can't both update the same patient record and I got locked out a couple of times.' He grinned at her.

'Right. Will do.' Hope pressed a couple of keys on the laptop, clearly saving and closing something, and shot him an impish look. 'Are you ready to go?'

'Absolutely.'

Theo threw her empty coffee cup into the bin, and put everything back in place, while Hope threaded her bag across her body so she had both hands free for her crutches. They took the small lift down to the ground floor, and he let her walk on her own down the ramp that led to the car park. She juggled a little with the crutches when she reached the open passenger door of his car, and Theo gave in and offered her his arm.

The big, well-kept house was protected from view by a deep rhododendron hedge full of buds, which were about to burst into bloom. Theo parked next to Hope's car, in front of the house, and she turned in her seat, seeming a little nervous.

'Would you like to come in for some tea? Or do you have to rush off?'

Theo wondered *where* Hope might possibly think he was rushing off to. Friday evenings weren't quite as full as they had been eighteen years ago, when there was always somewhere to go to celebrate the end of a long week.

'Tea would be nice, thank you.' He ignored the sudden craving for her company, concentrating on the idea that winding down for the weekend wasn't entirely possible until he'd seen Hope settled safely at home.

'Um… Right, then.' She seemed suddenly at a loss over the practicalities of getting back out of the car, and Theo hurried around to the passenger door to help her. As soon as she was on her feet again, she started to make for the paved pathway that led around to the kitchen at the back.

It was quiet here, the well-tended garden at the back surrounded by an old wall, which lent privacy and charm. Maybe a little too quiet, a little too secluded for Hope's peace of mind at the moment. She opened the back door, leading him into the open-plan kitchen living room.

'Shall I make the tea?'

Finally Hope smiled. 'Thanks for the offer but… go and sit down.' She gestured towards the seating area. 'Let me manage for myself.'

He could do that. Even if sinking into an armchair wasn't entirely relaxing, because every muscle in his body tensed when she reached for something or fumbled with her crutches. As soon as the tea was made, he felt justified in getting to his feet and carrying the two cups, while Hope followed. She sank down onto the sofa, opposite where he'd been sitting, and slipped off her shoe, propping both feet up on the cushions next to her.

'Ahh! That's better.' She reached for her tea and took a sip. 'It'll only be a couple of weeks, at most, before I can put some weight on my leg, and one crutch will be a lot easier than two.'

Theo nodded. The more she rested now, the sooner that would be, but he didn't need to tell Hope that. Something was still bothering her, though. He'd noticed that her hand shook a little as she picked up her cup. If anything, she seemed more nervous, more defensive, now that she was home.

Eighteen years suddenly felt like a very long time, as all the things that could happen to a person crowded in on him. All of the sorrows that a place might hold, which he could only guess at, but seemed written into the tension on her face.

'You have a lovely home.' The kitchen was modern and well equipped but welcoming as well. Everything that Theo wanted to create, in the family home that he so longed for.

'Thank you.' Hope pursed her lips thoughtfully, looking around her. 'I have a lot of good memories stored up in this house. Although I have to admit to feeling a little lonely here, since Mum died.'

He got that. Maybe it was time for him to stop thinking, and start saying. They'd never hesitated to tell each other what was on their minds before.

'Why would you have to admit to it, when that's perfectly normal? You've lost someone you love, and yesterday you fell and hurt yourself. If it was me, I'd be feeling very sorry for myself.'

Maybe he'd said too much, Hope stared at him, almost spilling her tea. But then she smiled. 'This is what I miss. Someone telling me what they really think. Mum always did that, even if it got very muddled towards the end of her life.'

Theo nodded. 'It's what I miss about Willow's teens, sometimes. She had no filters between what she thought and what she said. It prompted tears sometimes, not all of them hers, but...' He shrugged.

'Then she learnt tact?'

'Yeah. It's a lot less awkward, but thankfully she's not so good at it that it's a major problem.'

Hope was trembling again, and a tear appeared in the corner of one eye. She put down her mug, struggling to her feet, and Theo wondered whether he'd inadvertently been tactless.

'Are we going somewhere?' He was at a loss to know what to do next.

She nodded, and started to walk towards the door that led into the hallway. There was nothing else Theo could do but follow her.

Hope stopped at the bottom of the stairs, handing him one of her crutches and gripping the banister. The look on her face resembled that of a mountaineer, standing at the bottom of a precipice, trying to gauge what dangers the route ahead might hold.

'We'll do it this way.' He leant the crutch against the wall, moving behind her and slightly to the side, and coiling one arm around her waist. His other hand went to her shoulder, which felt suddenly anything but professional. Theo was about to loosen his grip and think of another way to get her up the stairs safely, when he felt Hope lean against him.

'That's good. Thank you, I feel a lot more stable.'

And he felt... Protective. Determined to keep her safe and so, so happy that she wasn't fighting him. 'Off you go, then. One at a time...'

CHAPTER SIX

THIS HADN'T BEEN as hard as Hope had thought it might be, but that didn't mean it was anything approaching easy. Feeling Theo close helped, though. Knowing that he'd catch her if she fell, and hoping that he might know what to do when she ripped the dustcovers off her biggest secret.

She wobbled a bit, halfway up the stairs, and felt his grip tighten around her waist. Breathtakingly strong and solid. 'Okay?'

Not really. She'd seen all kinds of human frailty in her time as a doctor, and she knew that Theo had too. The hoard was something he could treat with understanding, just as she'd understood when she'd realised a patient was in this situation. But could Theo understand why she'd kept it a secret for so long?

'I'm fine. Keep going.'

They made the top of the stairs, and he guided her towards the row of six storage boxes, stacked two high against the wall. Hope turned her face away from him, wondering if this was the moment she dreaded.

But instead of wanting to know what was in them, he leaned down pressing his hand on the top of one of them. 'These okay to sit on, while I fetch your other crutch?'

She let out a breath. 'Yes. They're not going to

collapse.' They were full of old newspapers and would easily support her weight. Hope sat down, watching as he hurried down the stairs, and then back up again.

He handed her the second crutch, and then sat down on the two boxes next to hers. Hope took a breath.

'When I fell yesterday… I should have asked you to help me bring the table downstairs, but I couldn't. No one's allowed up here.'

Theo nodded slowly, obviously going through all of the options in his head. 'How long?'

'Since I was seven. Mum and Dad always used to organise a big birthday party for me, they'd put a tent up in the garden…' The memory of those sunshiny days hurt, and she brushed away a tear. 'They had the main bedroom and mine was the second biggest. The others had…things we didn't use, stored in boxes. Old furniture. One of my friends came up here, and when her Mum came to collect her she told her that she'd seen…'

He was beginning to understand. 'What happened?'

Hope shrugged. 'Mum looked really embarrassed and my friend's mother shushed her and told her to be quiet. I thought everyone had rooms like that in their house, and it was the first time I realised that ours was different and I had to keep it a secret. So I did, and whenever I had friends round after that, Mum used to lock the doors of the back bedrooms.'

'And…the rest of the house?' Theo enquired, gently.

'It was a little full. Quite cluttered, if I'm honest, but my dad loved all kinds of interesting things and I grew up surrounded by treasures. When Dad died, Mum didn't want to sleep upstairs any more, and so I helped her move her bedroom downstairs. I reorganised and boxed up a lot of things we didn't need and put them upstairs. She wouldn't think of letting me throw anything away, but I had to give her a safe, ordered environment. When we needed carers to come in for her, I locked all of the upstairs rooms and told them that I'd closed them up because the house was too big and Mum couldn't manage the stairs.'

'Hope, you did everything you could for your mum. You didn't force her to throw things away, and you provided her with a safe living space. It must have been hard for you.'

Theo had reacted just as she'd expected. He'd listened and he hadn't judged. But sooner or later he'd start to make the connections she dreaded. 'Remember Andrew Locke? How you said that the hardest thing was that no one knew he was using cocaine?'

'That's not the same thing, Hope. He was putting himself at risk—'

Theo stopped, shaking his head as Hope looked

down at her orthopaedic boot. 'That's the wrong answer, isn't it? How about the answer I don't want to give, because I find it really hard? We all like to pretend that everything's under control. I did when Jonas died, but in fact I was sitting, staring at a blank wall every evening, not eating or sleeping. It took six months of therapy before I could even talk about it.'

'That's been your secret?' Suddenly everything shifted. Despite her aches and pains, and all of the fear she'd felt over bringing Theo up here, Hope felt strong again. She wanted to be strong, for Theo.

'Yeah. And this is yours. But we're both doing our best to move forward and remake our lives.'

Hope thought for a moment. 'Thank you for telling me, Theo. I knew your change in direction was important for you, but I didn't realise how important.'

'Because I didn't tell you. We should have told each other about these things, but we didn't and that's okay, because we're both human.' He reached down, tapping one of the boxes beneath them. 'So... What exactly am I sitting on?'

'Take a look.' Theo clearly couldn't talk any more about Jonas, but if Hope could be open with him about her own issues then that might help him to trust her with his.

Theo got to his feet, lifting off the hard plastic

cover and reading the banner on the newspaper inside. '*The Hastings Weekly Digest.*'

'Yes, my dad used to get it every week. Even when he wasn't well, he'd go out to the newsagent for his copy.'

'And they're all in sequence?'

Hope nodded. She probably shouldn't care about that—she never looked at the newspapers. But her dad had always kept them carefully folded and in date order. Suddenly she didn't want Theo to disturb them.

'I'd love to see them some time. Not now, though, they're filed away so neatly.' He understood without having to ask.

'You can look in the bedrooms. The keys are in the lock box on the wall.' She pointed to the small key safe, reciting the combination.

Theo fetched the keys and then opened the doors of all four bedrooms in turn. Then he came back to sit down next to her, his brow creased in thought.

'There's...it's a lot of memories.'

At least he hadn't said *rubbish*. Hope nodded. 'That isn't all. The loft's been boarded out and there's a lot up there as well. It all feels...there's so much of it.'

'When someone dies, going through their things is really hard. Maybe this is a version of Willow's trunk and you have to keep these things until you're ready to let some of them go.'

'It's a bit bigger than Willow's trunk. Dad had

extra beams put into the floors up here when I was little…'

'That's sensible.'

Theo's reaction made her smile. 'Nothing about this is sensible, Theo.'

'Not sensible maybe, but it makes sense.' He sat down next to her again. 'You'll work it out, Hope. And if you want me to help you with any of it, then you know where I am.'

'Thank you for not fainting with shock.' She smiled up at him.

'There's still time. You haven't got a basement, have you?'

Theo had always been able to make her laugh, and she appreciated that now more than she ever had. 'No. I do have a potting shed, full of garden equipment. Some of which is broken.'

'Since that's not actually *in* the house, would it be splitting hairs to ask how you feel about that?' He grinned.

'Theo! Yes, it would be splitting hairs. Although you have a point. I'm not sure I feel quite the same about three or four broken lawnmowers. Dad hated gardening, and after things got a bit out of control, he got someone in to keep the garden neat.'

'There you go, then. Perhaps that's the place to start.'

A start. The thought made her almost giddy with elation. Hope got to her feet, almost losing her balance as her crutch slipped out of her hand, rolling onto the floor. But Theo was there, steadying her.

Suddenly she was caught in his gaze. Lost in his smile. 'Careful…' The word seemed to form the shape of a kiss, and Hope shivered.

'Let's both be careful. We'll look after each other's dreams.' They both knew how important those dreams were, now, because Hope had shared her secret and Theo had shared his.

'That works for me. Thanks for listening, Hope.'

'I'd like to listen some more. Whenever you're ready.' Hope sensed that Theo wasn't ready yet, but she'd be there for him when he was. 'In the meantime, shall we start by taking it carefully down the stairs?'

Theo chuckled. 'Absolutely. Then I may insist you sit down, while I cook for you.'

'You cook?'

'Of course I do. How do you suppose I've eaten for all these years? I upped my game a little when Carrie left, Willow and I made a thing of going to markets together and learning to cook dishes from whichever country we were in. Mexico was a big success for us.'

'Can you make tacos?'

Theo chuckled. 'Can I make tacos? Our next-door neighbour taught us. One taste of her special seasoning and you'll never look at the tacos you get at the supermarket again.'

'You're full of surprises, Theo. But I don't have

anything in the fridge, so we'll have to make do
with a takeaway.'

'Sounds good. I'll bring some things over tomorrow and cook then, instead.'

'You're cooking me dinner tomorrow?' Hope
smiled at him, forgetting all about the resolution
she'd made to manage for herself. 'That's nice...'

Four terms. Eighteen years. Two weeks. How did
they add up to what he and Hope had now?

Theo wasn't sure. The four terms that they'd
spent together had been a blossoming. Their
friendship had grown into an easy relationship
where they could share anything. When he thought
about it their one kiss hadn't been a mistake, but
a natural progression of a relationship that could
no longer be contained within the boundaries of
friendship.

The eighteen years—life had intruded and
they'd followed different paths. If asked, Theo
would have answered that he'd made his mistakes,
but on balance he would have made the same decisions. He guessed that Hope's answer would be
the same.

And now, two precious, head-spinning weeks.
Both older and wiser, and carrying a lot more baggage. The friendship—that instant connection—
was still there, but their different lives had left
them needing very different things.

But this wasn't the time for equations. Hope had

to take some time to heal, and Theo would be there for her. Everything else could wait.

He was up early the following morning, and had shopped for two in the supermarket, stopping off to fill his own fridge before going on to Hope's place. He found her standing in the open doorway of the potting shed, regarding its contents. It was so full that it was going to be necessary to take some things out before it was possible for either of them to go inside.

'What do you think?' Her voice trembled slightly. This wasn't going to be as easy for her as she'd made out yesterday.

'I think it'll take a while to do this properly.'

She shot him a helpless look. 'Properly?'

This wasn't like Hope at all. She was one of the most capable people he knew, but somehow her parents' possessions seemed to strip her of all of her resourcefulness and leave her lost and vulnerable.

'I imagine there are some things there that you'll want to keep. I can see some gardening tools over there in the corner that look to be in good condition. There may be some chemicals that have been banned now, and so the best thing to do with them is find out how they can be disposed of safely. Then for the things you don't need, we can find out about recycling or reuse. I'd be surprised if too much has to be thrown away.'

She nodded. 'That sounds good. I'd like to put

as much as possible to some use, even if it's just recycling. I can get started on that today, and do it bit by bit.'

'Would you like a hand? It'll go quicker with two.' And easier, probably. Hope knew exactly what she wanted, but she seemed to need someone to give her permission to go ahead and make it happen.

'Don't you have your own things to be getting on with?' Hope looked at him thoughtfully and Theo avoided her gaze.

'They'll keep. Since I'm here now, with all the ingredients for tacos, then the least we could do is work up a bit of an appetite…'

CHAPTER SEVEN

EVERYONE AT THE Arrow Lane medical centre had rallied round. He and Sara Jamieson were covering Hope's home visits. Terri, the receptionist, fetched and carried for her, usually before Hope had even asked for something, and Rosie swung into a fierce but smiling organisational mode, making sure that everything ran like clockwork. Rosie picked Hope up on her way to work in the mornings, and Theo claimed the right to take her home again, sometimes staying to cook, and sometimes leaving when Hope chased him away.

It wasn't permanent but it was a comfortable routine that supported Theo as much as it did Hope. He'd almost managed to forget that he'd spoken about Jonas and he'd pushed those feelings to the back of his mind, where they couldn't hurt him.

'Theo, we need you in Reception. It's an emergency.' Rosie's voice was level and calm, which told Theo that he should hurry.

Before he'd made it downstairs he heard a baby screaming. The reception area was empty, and Rosie was on the phone. A young woman lay on the carpeted floor, her feet propped up on a couple of cushions, and Hope was kneeling awkwardly beside her.

'Bee sting. She's in anaphylactic shock…' Hope's

voice was calm as well, and the emergency rating in Theo's head ratcheted up a notch. An empty handbag was lying on the floor, along with a mess of contents, and Hope was holding an epinephrine auto-injector, the orange needle cover extended, indicating that it had just been used.

He took the auto-injector from her hand, and Hope nodded, picking up the second one that lay on the floor beside her and leaning over to catch the woman's attention.

'Tina… Tina, look at me. Gracie's all right, she's safe in her pram. She's just crying. Try to relax.'

To be fair, the baby didn't sound all right, and her cries were obviously agitating Tina. Theo knelt down beside her. 'The bee sting's out?'

Hope nodded. Tina was still very pale and struggling to breathe, and there was a bright red swelling on her left arm, obviously where she had been stung. She didn't seem to be responding to the first dose of epinephrine as well as they might have expected.

'We'll sit her up for a minute?' Theo suggested.

'Yes, that may help.' Hope shifted towards Tina's shoulders and together they helped her sit up. 'Is that helping you breathe, Tina?'

Tina shook her head, the wheezing in the back of her throat getting worse as she tried to reach for her baby. Everyone else was busy, Rosie was on the phone to the emergency services, and Terri was shepherding patients who were already in the building out, and making sure no one else entered.

'It's been more than five minutes. I may have to give her another shot of epinephrine.' Hope inclined her head towards the screaming baby in her pram and Theo nodded. Keeping her quiet couldn't do any harm and it might help her mother to relax and breathe.

He got to his feet, greeting the baby with a smile, and gently taking her from her pram. Theo started to sing quietly, and suddenly little Gracie stopped crying, looking up at him. He rocked her in time with the song and Gracie joined in with a few baby moves, waving her arms at him.

Out of the corner of his eye he saw Rosie grinning, the phone still pressed tightly to her ear. He turned to glance at Hope, who was smiling as well as she reassured Tina.

'There, see? I think Gracie's just made a new friend. I want you to try and relax if you can.'

The painful wheeze seemed to ease a bit and Hope helped Tina to lie back down again. But it wasn't enough. Hope was checking Tina's heart rate and breathing, and clearly wasn't happy with the situation. She administered a second shot of epinephrine and after a minute of silence, broken only by Hope's quiet reassurances, Tina's chest heaved as she sucked in a breath.

The relief was almost palpable. Gracie started to fret in his arms, and Theo quieted her, moving around to allow Tina to see her child. Feeling that tiny body move against him, breathing in the gorgeous baby scent, would make anyone relax and he couldn't help smiling. Hope grinned, telling Tina again that Gracie was fine and monitoring her recovery.

When the ambulance arrived, Tina was better still, but she still needed careful observation at the hospital to make sure her symptoms didn't return. Rosie handed over a printed set of patient notes, which included a written record of the treatment Tina had received this morning, and the paramedic turned to Theo.

'Wish all our calls went this smoothly. You're the father…?'

'Um… No.' He could see Rosie hiding a smile behind her hand and shot her a querying look. 'What's happening with Gracie?'

'I called Tina's partner and he's on his way to pick Gracie up. I said we were managing.'

'Thanks. We'll keep the baby here until then.' Maybe calling Gracie *the baby* would instil a note of professionalism into the situation, but when he looked back down at her Theo couldn't help falling in love all over again. 'I'll be upstairs.'

He stopped, to let Tina say goodbye to her daughter, and to reassure her that he'd take the best care of Gracie until her father arrived. Then Theo retreated to his consulting room, where he could sing his entire repertoire of Elvis Presley's greatest hits without interruption.

Hope had seen a new side of Theo. He was first and foremost a doctor, but he'd seen that she had the medical aspects in hand and done what was most needed to calm Tina down, and quietened Gracie. It was just a matter of practicality, wasn't it?

But there was nothing practical about the besotted smile he'd given Gracie. That was all Theo's rock-steady heart, which had been captured by a pair of blue eyes and shock of red-blonde hair. Seeing him with the baby had prompted two opposing reactions in Hope. She'd wanted to go and hug him, to be a part of that simple warmth. But at the same time, the knowledge that this was what he wanted for himself, and it was something she might not be able to give him, had clawed at her.

Gracie's father arrived, and Theo brought the baby downstairs, handing her over. She started to fret, obviously missing him already, and Hope thought she saw a quick flash of longing in his eyes. Theo was clearly missing Gracie already as well, although he made a point of telling her father that thanks weren't needed, and he should get on his way to see Tina.

Theo retreated to his consulting room, and Hope stayed in Reception while Rosie consulted the list of patients for the afternoon.

'We gave them the option but it seems no one wanted to wait. I'll call round and rebook the appointments.'

Hope nodded. 'Okay. I'll stay late if anyone wants to come back this evening. Have I got ten minutes?'

'Your next patient's not due until after lunch—you've got half an hour. I might take a break myself, to get over how good Dr Lewis is with kids. He can have my two for the weekend any time he likes.'

Hope chuckled. It was going to take her a good deal more than half an hour to get over the sight of Theo crooning to Gracie. 'You might have a fight on your hands, getting them back again.'

Rosie laughed. 'Does he have kids of his own?'

'A daughter. She's twenty.' And he'd missed being a dad when Willow was a baby. Hope knew what it was like to miss out, and maybe it was time to give him a nudge. 'Take a break, Rosie, and make sure that Terri does too. You've earned it this morning. You were both brilliant and we couldn't have done without you.'

Despite having an orthopaedic boot and two crutches, Hope managed to give the impression of breezing into his office. Theo wasn't sure how she did that. Maybe it was something to do with her summer dress and her smile, which made him think of sunshine and a gentle, scented breath of wind.

She sat down, grinning at him. Maybe he was supposed to go first, but he wasn't entirely sure what was on her mind.

'All right. Spit it out.'

'I'm just wondering how I could have been so wrong about you, Theo.'

He raised his eyebrows. Hope was being extra-ambiguous, which meant he was probably in for a telling-off about something. He'd better get it over with.

'Cut to the chase, Hope. Haven't we got a whole roomful of people downstairs that we need to see?'

'It seems they all decided to go home and come back later. I dare say we'll be working a bit late this evening. We don't often have emergencies here.'

'Is that it? You've decided we need a few more emergencies?'

'No, one was enough. I like the opportunity of getting to know my patients, and preventing things from happening to them.'

'Yeah. Me too. What was Tina doing here, anyway?'

'I'd only just seen her, to give Gracie a check-up. Apparently she went outside, and Terri heard her scream. A bee had flown into Gracie's pram and Tina was flapping it away from her and got stung. We all know that Tina carries an epinephrine auto-injector as a precaution—she was stung several times as a teenager.'

'This time was worse?' Theo asked. That was usually the case with this kind of allergy.

'Much worse. There was only localised swelling before and her consultant didn't think that immunotherapy was necessary. We'll see what the hospital says this time around, but I think they may offer it to her.'

Theo nodded. 'I imagine she's probably got used to just stepping away when she sees a bee. But she was trying to protect Gracie.'

'Yes. I think that's exactly what she was trying to do. Theo, I can handle Tina's ongoing care. What I came to say…' She stopped short as he chuckled. 'What?'

'Go on. Don't let me stop you now.'

Hope shot him an injured look. 'What I came to say is that I'm so grateful for all you've done in the last couple of weeks. You've been amazing. I'm just concerned and I'd really like you to spend some more time looking after yourself.'

'What brought this on?' Theo thought he knew. Gracie had slid in under all of his defences and allowed him to think that he could have the life he wanted. Settled and fulfilled. Maybe even a family…

She shrugged. 'You've been through a lot, Theo. You told me that you were looking to settle, and build up a supportive framework, but you're not doing anything about it.'

Hope underestimated herself. She was insightful

and unerring in her aim when she wanted to be. Theo wondered if she knew that he'd been imagining a baby that looked just like her in his arms, and decided that was beyond even her capabilities.

'It'll happen.'

'No, it won't. Not if you don't make it.'

Suddenly, in Hope's clear gaze, it all seemed so obvious. He *did* need a home, a place of strength from which he could reach out. 'I guess I could go and look at a few houses, just to get a feel for what I want. Scan the situations vacant columns.' None of that seemed terribly appealing.

'You want a hand with it? I don't have much experience with either of those things so you'd need to contribute all the opinions. I'll just listen and agree with whatever you say.'

Theo chuckled. Suddenly house-hunting and job-hunting didn't seem quite so bad. 'I'm definitely taking you up on that, Hope. I'm not passing up the chance to watch you agreeing with everything I say.'

'I might be asking a few pertinent questions, though.' She shot him a grin that made her green eyes dance with mischief. Suddenly everything he wanted seemed like a possibility.

'I wouldn't expect anything less.' He looked at his watch. 'We *will* come back to this, but you're probably as hungry as I am, and we've got a long afternoon ahead of us. What do you say I pop out and get sandwiches?'

'Good idea. You'll find me in my consulting room, laying plans for your future.'

Theo chuckled. As long as Hope intended to include herself in those plans, she'd get no arguments from him.

They were making a slightly different routine. Saturday mornings were devoted to finding him a permanent job and a place to live, and Hope's enthusiasm for the task had convinced Theo to at least consider several options. Then he cooked, using one of the recipes he and Willow had most enjoyed on their travels. They'd been to Mexico, Italy and then India, and by the time they got to Germany Hope was moving around more easily, putting weight on her injured ankle and using just one crutch.

Theo had been waiting for a good moment to broach the subject, and when they retired to the sitting room to finish off glasses of German beer with their coffee, now seemed as good a time as any.

'I've been thinking. About your collection...'

A flash of panic showed in her eyes. Hope had gradually got the message that the secret hoard above their heads was nothing to be ashamed of, but she was still protective of the memories that were stored upstairs. All of her old dresses and toys from when she was little. Stones from trips to the beach, all boxed up and labelled with the date. A whole wardrobe full of things saved from her parents' wedding.

She hesitated, but Theo knew that curiosity would win out in the end. 'Okay. What are you thinking?'

'I did some digging, and there's a project based in Eastbourne, which collects all kinds of documents and scans them. The plan is to make them accessible to everyone on the Internet, and they're sharing the scans with local records offices to make them as widely available as possible.'

Hope thought for a moment. 'What happens… afterwards?'

'After they're scanned? They'll give them back to you, I suppose.'

'What?' Her eyes widened. 'No, that's not going to work for me, Theo. I *told* you, when you asked whether I was regretting giving Willow the lamp, that if I can find a good home for something, I'm never going to allow it back in the house.'

Theo had reckoned that might be a step too far with her father's newspapers. 'They're in touch with several different physical archives, and they'll find a home for things.'

'Newspapers? Photographs?'

'Photographs?'

She puffed out a breath. 'There are a couple of boxes of old photographic plates that Dad got from a shop that was closing down. Views of old Hastings, that kind of thing.'

'I don't know. We could take a look at their website.'

Hope got up from her chair, and Theo resisted the impulse to help her. He always received the same impatient wave of her hand when he tried that, and had to admit that helping her was often a matter of his own pleasure in feeling her close. She fetched her tablet from its place under the TV, and tapped the screen, handing it to him before sitting down on the sofa next to him. Theo called up the website and felt Hope lean against his arm as she craned to see over his shoulder.

'It says…yeah, they can scan photographs and any negatives or photographic plates. Ah, and see here. They credit anyone who's given them anything.'

'Let me see…' Hope grabbed the tablet from him, navigating to the credits page. 'That's really nice. Do you think they'd put my dad's name on there?'

'I'd imagine they'll put any name you like. They have an open day at one of the libraries in Eastbourne every Sunday, where people can go and talk to someone about the project. You could ask them yourself.'

'Yes, that's a good idea. I'll go…' Hope frowned down at the boot on her leg. 'When I can drive over there.'

Too much time to think about things generally meant that Hope sank back into the despair of looking at the whole task and finding it too much to contemplate. Picking off one job at a time gave her a boost of success. 'We could go tomorrow. The estate agent I saw last week gave me a list of different local areas, and said I should rate them in order of preference. Since I don't know any of them it's difficult, so I thought I might have a tour round and see what they're like.'

'Sounds good. You obviously like this one a lot better than the last two you went to see.'

'Yeah, I do. She hasn't suggested any underhand ways of knocking the asking price down yet, which is a definite point in her favour. I might even marry her—that would knock two items off my to-do list.' Theo was joking, but he couldn't help liking the way Hope shot him a disapproving look when he mentioned marriage. Lately it had been her smile that had welcomed him home in the dream-like visions of the life he wanted.

'You're not taking this too seriously, are you, Theo?'

'I'm taking the job and somewhere to live seriously. Maybe I'm a little too set in my ways to consider dating as something that needs to be project-managed.'

'Have you been texting Willow again?' Hope grinned.

'Yeah. She sent me a questionnaire she found, and I only got four out of thirty. I'm clearly not great partner material.'

The way Hope looked him up and down made his fingertips tingle. There was something about the coolly assessing look of an intelligent, beautiful woman that was a real turn-on.

'I don't know. You're good-looking. Great sense of humour. Kind.' A trace of mischief showed in her smile. '*Very* charming.'

'Thank you. You make me sound far nicer than I actually am.'

'No, you're far nicer than you think.'

Theo sighed. 'What about you, then? Any plans?'

Her lovely eyes focussed suddenly on his face. 'Tick-tock, Theo.'

He shook his head. 'What does that mean? You're thirty-nine. You still have time for a family, if that's what you want.'

'It's not that simple.' She turned her gaze onto him. 'You've had relationships in the last eighteen years?'

'You know I have. Not so much after Carrie left, but that was because I wanted to provide a stable home environment for Willow. Even if she did have other ideas, and developed a habit of playing matchmaker.' Then it hit him. Hope had always seemed so comfortable in her skin, so at home with being an attractive woman. She was capable of flirting mercilessly with him and he'd assumed...

'It's been different for me. I dated a bit while I was doing my foundation training, but even then

I didn't have the time for relationships to get too serious, and when I moved in with Mum that was an end to that side of things.'

Theo swallowed hard. 'You mean…?'

'Theo!' She dug her fingers into his ribs and he jumped. 'I know what sex is, and I've been there and tried it. More than once. I just never had those years when I was free to explore how I wanted to live my life. I've got the opportunity to do that now, in lots of different ways. Maybe I'll take a year's sabbatical from work and go travelling. Maybe I won't, but I have the opportunity to make those decisions now.'

Theo frowned. He should have seen it, but he'd been too busy thinking about himself. How Hope was the woman he'd been looking for all of these years. He'd turned his back on the obvious truth—that she'd never been in any position to look.

'So you're planning on making a few mistakes, are you?' He *really* didn't like that idea. Theo didn't care if he made a fool of himself by betraying his feelings, he'd put up a fight to keep her from hurt.

'I've been in general practice and looking after my mum for most of the last eighteen years, and both of those things teach you a fair bit about human nature. So no, mistakes definitely aren't on my bucket list. But you've had the opportunity to explore and try things out. Can't you see that's what I need?'

He could see it. And maybe *he* needed to do a bit of growing up if he thought that their differences were just a matter of circumstance—Hope had the emotional maturity to know that it was more than that, and she understood that it might be too late for her to have a family before she got to the point of wanting to settle down.

'You're a very smart cookie.'

She chuckled. 'I'm just facing the facts.'

Putting his arm around her shoulders seemed suddenly like crossing a line that had just been drawn between them. Hope saw his hesitancy and bumped her shoulder against his, smiling. So Theo threw caution to the winds and did it anyway.

'Are we okay?' Hope's question reminded him that she must know there was a little more than 'just friends' to their relationship. Even if wanting more would never allow them to lead the lives they wanted.

'We're always okay, aren't we?'

Every step with Theo was a risk. Every secret, each admission. But Hope had to accept that he was the one who got away, and that they were too different now to be anything other than fond friends. That reward made her bold enough—or maybe foolish enough—to take any risk. And each time he'd come through for her. That was what friendship was all about, wasn't it?

'I have a plan forming.'

He chuckled. 'Go on, then. Give it some room to breathe.'

'The table that I brought down from the loft… would it have done for Willow's room, beside her bed?'

Theo thought for a moment. 'Yeah, it would have done very well. You want me to see if I can put it back together?'

She couldn't help rolling her eyes. 'Theo, I'm quite capable of noticing that something's broken, and that one's marked for recycling. But there are two more in the loft, along with some other bits and pieces. Picture frames, and so on…'

'No, Hope. You are *not* going back up into the loft. If I have to kidnap you and lock you in my flat until Monday morning, then I will.'

'Goes without saying. I was actually thinking that you might go up there. I'll just stand at the bottom of the ladder and shout a few helpful suggestions.'

He nodded. 'Okay. I can get behind that as a plan.'

Having him follow her up the stairs, there in case she lost her balance, gave her time to think. And waiting on the landing listening to him moving things around in the loft gave her even more time. Then he appeared in the opening at the top of the steps, and his smile told her that this new foray into her family's secrets hadn't been a mistake.

'Do people *really* collect this much furniture?'

'We did. Dad and Mum married a little late in life, and so they both had their own places already. This house used to belong to an old lady who'd died, and a load of furniture came with it. Then there were the things that they bought together.'

He nodded. 'That accounts for it. You have some nice things up here.'

'Dad always used to say that they'd come in handy some time. They just never did.' Hope frowned, feeling a tug of regret.

'He was right. I found the tables and one of them will be perfect for Willow's room. It just needs to be cleaned up a bit.'

That made her feel a great deal better. 'Now it's just a matter of finding somewhere for all the rest of it.'

'One thing at a time. You don't need to do everything at once, you just need to make a little progress in the direction you want to go.'

'Stop being so wise, Theo, and get on with it. There are some picture frames over to the left, above the front bedroom, I think.'

Theo brought the table down from the loft, along with a box of picture frames, which was a great deal larger than she remembered it. He took everything down to the kitchen to be cleaned up and while Hope was looking under the sink for a tin of wax polish, he found treasure.

'Hope. You *have* to keep these.'

'I thought the whole idea was *not* keeping

things…' She turned and caught sight of the partially unwrapped frames. 'Oh! I think I remember them.'

'You do?'

'Yes, my grandad had something like this in his sitting room. I think he might have made them himself. He was a carpenter.'

Theo laid the frames carefully on the kitchen table, and left Hope to tear at the wrappings. Neither frame was damaged, and they looked like the ones she remembered. She studied them carefully and found what she was looking for.

'See, in the corner here. Those are his initials: *AA*.'

'And this one?' Theo indicated a pair of initials on the other frame. *MA*.

'That's my grandmother. Albert and Margaret. And look, what's this underneath?'

Theo went to the sink to fetch a damp cloth, and handed it to her. Hope carefully cleaned away the accumulation of debris under the initials. 'It says… looks like a nineteen…and then "October 1932". Theo, I think that's when they got married. Do you think he made them for her, as a wedding present?'

'Can you check?' Theo's face reflected the same excitement of discovery that she felt.

'There's a photograph album in the sitting room. In the glass-fronted cabinet…'

'I'll go and fetch it. See if you can clean the frame up a bit more.'

It took half an hour to find the photograph and reveal the lettering on both frames. But when they had, everything became clear. The date on the back of her grandparents' wedding-day photograph matched the one carved onto the frame. And then Theo looked again at the photograph.

'Look, isn't that these frames on the wall behind them?'

Hope had looked at the photograph hundreds of times before, but that detail had been hiding in plain sight. 'Yes, I think it is. I'm so glad we've found these, Theo. It's not all about throwing things away, is it?'

He grinned. 'No, it's about taking ownership of the things that mean something to you. Thinking about it, that might be the next thing on my to-do list as well. Finding a place that means something to me and taking ownership of it…'

CHAPTER EIGHT

THE LAST COUPLE of weeks hadn't been easy. They'd both been on edge, unsure of the changes they were making, and that had caused a few arguments, when either Theo pushed a little too hard, or Hope did. But her ankle was feeling much stronger now, and she could walk around indoors without crutches, although she still needed one if she was on her feet too much. The black bruises on her back and side were fading, and she'd be able to drive her own car soon, instead of relying on lifts and taxis.

And Theo had stuck with her. After speaking to the woman in charge of the scanning project, in Eastbourne, Hope had decided that this was where she wanted her dad's newspapers to go. It had been a difficult process, but Theo had been patient, taking scans of all the articles she wanted to keep, before she folded each paper back into the box. And today, they'd be delivering the boxes. Hope wasn't entirely sure how she'd feel when it got to the moment of handing them over, but she knew for sure that it was what she wanted to do.

Theo tapped on the kitchen door at eight in the morning. The boxes of newspapers and photographic plates were still upstairs, waiting for him to carry them down to his car.

'Hey.' He sat down at the kitchen table with her.

'How do you feel? I could do with a coffee before we get started.'

That was nice of him. Hope could do with a moment, too. 'Toast?'

'Yes please, if you're making some.' He reached into his pocket as his phone rang, and Hope got up from the table to make the toast.

'Willow. Willow, stop for a moment and take a breath. Where are you now? Okay, that's good. Do you have someone with you? Let me speak to them.'

That didn't sound good. Hope turned, and the look in Theo's eyes told her that there was definitely something wrong.

'Hi, Phoebe. Thanks so much for looking after Willow. I'll be there in an hour. Would you be able to stay? Thank you. If she seems drowsy...'

Someone spoke at the other end of the line and Theo smiled suddenly. 'That's great, then you know what to look for. Call me if you're at all worried about her... Yes, thanks.'

The phone was obviously passed back to Willow, and Theo told his daughter that he loved her, and he'd be there soon. Then he looked up at Hope.

'I'm so sorry. It's Willow, it sounds as if someone spiked her drink last night. A couple of her friends went home with her, but she's pretty shaken up. One of the girls she lives with, Phoebe, is a medical student and she seems to have everything under control, but I have to go...'

'Yes, of course.' Hope wondered whether she was overstepping their boundaries, but at the moment she didn't much care. 'I'll come with you.'

Theo hesitated. 'I'd love you to, but I think this is going to take a while.'

'Does she need to be examined by a doctor? She needs you to be her father, right now.'

Theo stared at her. 'Do you think...?'

'I don't think anything at the moment. From what you say, it sounds as if her friends were looking out for her and she hasn't been assaulted. But whatever's happened, Willow may want to talk to someone and I'm really sorry to have to say it, but that someone might not be you.'

He thought for a moment. 'You're right. I'd be so grateful, Hope. If someone has to examine her I'd rather it was you.'

'Don't stand around being grateful, go and get my doctor's bag. It's in the cupboard underneath the stairs. And bring one of my crutches—they're in the hall as well. You've got Phoebe's number?'

'Yes, she's texting it to me.' Theo was already on his way out of the kitchen, and Hope picked up his phone, copying the number on the text that had just arrived into her own phone.

She collected her bag, and Theo brought her jacket through from the hall. Hope was wondering whether she might need Theo to take a few breaths before he got into the car, but he was suddenly icy cool. She'd seen that before, Theo was taking a step back from his emotions, and concentrating on what needed to be done.

As they neared Brighton, Hope called Phoebe, introducing herself and asking for more details about what had happened. Theo turned into the car park for a small group of purpose-built houses, switched off the engine and leaned back in his seat.

'Okay. Before I go in with a thousand questions, what did Phoebe say?'

'Willow's okay.' She started with the news that Theo really needed to hear. 'Apparently she went out with a group of friends last night. They all live together?'

'Yeah, that's right. The university owns these houses and they rent them out to second- and third-year groups of students.'

'They went to a bar, down by the beach, and Phoebe found Willow in the open-air area in front of the bar. She said she was feeling really tired and wanted to go home. Phoebe said she'd go with her, it was getting late and she was tired too, and they got a taxi back here with another girl. Willow just went to her room, and they thought she was okay.'

'She wasn't…' Theo waved his hand, unable to ask the question out loud.

'Her clothes weren't torn, and she didn't say anything about being attacked. They have trackers on their phones apparently and when Phoebe checked Willow's location history, she hadn't been off the premises. She says the open-air part of the bar is pretty crowded on a Friday evening. There are always plenty of people around.'

'Okay, thanks. So how did they know anything was up?'

'Willow banged on Phoebe's door, early this morning, saying she had a splitting headache and couldn't remember anything from last night. They knew that Willow hadn't been drunk—they'd been together for most of the evening and Willow was drinking orange juice and lemonade. So they calmed her down a bit and called you.'

'We'll need to have her seen by a doctor...' Theo shook his head. 'That's us, isn't it?'

'It's me, yes. But—one more thing—Phoebe's feeling really bad about this. She told me that she should have known that something had happened—'

'No. No, you can't always tell. Even if you *are* a third-year medical student.'

Hope nodded. 'Well, I think that message might sink in a little better if it came from you.'

'Got it. Can we go in now?'

Theo had left the car keys in the ignition and hurried ahead of Hope, leaving her behind. A young black woman answered the door, exchanging a few words with Theo before standing to one side to let him into the house and then waiting for Hope to catch up.

'Hi, I'm Phoebe. You're Hope?'

'Yes. Thanks for waiting for me. Theo seems to have forgotten all about my doctor's bag. I don't suppose you could help me with it, could you?'

Phoebe smiled. 'Give me the keys, I'll go and get it for you. What did you do?'

'It's a Weber A fracture.'

'Ah, yes. I know what that is. It must be great for Willow, having two parents who are doctors.'

Hope chuckled. 'I'm not Theo's partner, I'm just a colleague. Personally, I think one doctor's bad enough. He knows far too much about what could happen in any given situation.'

'He's much calmer than *my* dad would have been.'

'Trust me, he's nowhere near calm. If Willow wants to talk to me alone, then I'm relying on you…' Hope saw Phoebe's look of uncertainty and caught her arm.

'Listen, Phoebe, this is important. Theo knows that it's not always easy to spot when someone's drink has been spiked. And he's grateful that you all look after each other when you go out together. It sounds as if the situation that Willow was in last night had the potential for all kinds of harm to come to her, and it was your rules that kept her safe.'

Phoebe had been studying the ground between them, but when she looked up at Hope she was smiling. 'Thanks for that. Stay here, I'll go and fetch your things.'

'It's the nylon bag, in the boot. Next to the box of picture frames…'

* * *

The student houses had a kitchen and sitting room on the ground floor, with eight bedrooms on two floors above that. Someone, Phoebe probably, had taken charge of the situation, and the group of young women huddled together at the kitchen table looked up at them as they passed but said nothing. At the top of the stairs another of the house residents, who appeared to be standing guard, scooted out of the way to let them past.

'Hey, Willow.' Phoebe's first words were for her adoptive patient, and Hope nodded her on. She was handling this in exactly the right way. 'Look who's here. It's Hope.'

Theo was sitting on the bed, a bundle of red corkscrew curls wrapped in a colourful quilt in his arms. A pale freckled face, streaked with tears, looked up at them, and Hope wondered fleetingly whether Willow would even know what she was doing here.

Willow managed a fragile smile. 'I've heard all about you.'

'I sent Willow some pictures of the lamp you gave her...' Theo added hastily, in an obvious attempt to give the impression that Willow hadn't heard *all* about her. 'I think she'd like to talk to you. Is that right, sweetheart?'

'Yes, Dad. That's what I want.' There was a hint of firmness in Willow's tone, and Hope smiled.

Clearly the two of them had already worked that out between them.

'Okay, well…' Theo seemed disinclined to let Willow go, and Phoebe stepped in.

'I bet you could do with a cup of tea, Dr Lewis. Come and sit in my room. It's just next door.'

Theo still didn't move, and Hope pulled a chair from the desk on the other side of the room, sitting down opposite them. 'Theo…'

'Yeah. Right.' Theo shot her a smile and let go of his daughter. 'I'll be right here, Willow…'

'I know, Dad.'

Phoebe hustled Theo out of the room, closing the door behind them. Willow watched them go, pulling at the sleeve of her grey sweatshirt. 'He's a bit…'

Overprotective? Hope had been on the receiving end of that and it wasn't so bad. Terrified for his daughter? That just made Theo human. 'He just wants to be here, for you.'

'Yeah, I know. Dad's really good about things, on the whole.'

'I imagine so.'

That was the first question covered, and they could move on to the more difficult ones now. 'Look, Willow, you're in charge of everything that happens next. You can say whatever you want to me, and it won't go any further. That includes your dad. He knows I won't be telling him anything that you haven't specifically asked me to.'

Willow shook her head, miserably. 'That's the problem. I don't know what happened.'

'What do you remember?'

Willow's eyes filled with tears. 'Going out, being in the bar. I was feeling a bit hot and dizzy and then… I woke up, this morning. I didn't even know how I got here, until Phoebe told me. I don't know what happened to me.'

Hope reached forward, taking Willow's hand. 'Okay, honey. I imagine that's a really difficult thing to think about. If you want me to, I can find out how you are now.'

Willow nodded. 'Yes. I'm not sure I *want* to know, but I think I need to.'

'All right. There are a number of things we can do together. I can look at your clothes, and examine you for any bruises or injuries. I have a test kit in my bag and if you want we can do a urine test to find out a little bit more about any drugs that are still in your system…' Hope skimmed over the details, not wanting to make any assumptions.

'What about my blood?' Willow frowned. 'Do we have to report it to the police?'

'That's up to you, Willow. If you want to report this, then your dad and I will be with you all the way. If you don't then that's okay too. The thing is that any tests which I do are considered purely diagnostic, and not part of the chain of evidence, so they'd need to take their own blood sample.'

Willow nodded. 'I'm not sure… I don't even know if anything's happened for me to report.'

'That's fine. Why don't you think about it and tell me what you want later? But there's one thing that I do want you to know. We suspect that someone might have spiked your drink, yes?'

Willow nodded.

'Well, if they have, that's a crime—something that's been done to you without your consent. You couldn't have done anything about it, and it's not your fault.'

'I bet Dad's thinking that I could have been a bit more careful.' A tear rolled down Willow's cheek.

'No, he isn't. He knows the score on this, probably better than most people. I promise you, Willow, Theo's not going to blame you…'

Maybe that betrayed a little too much about Hope's relationship with Theo. But she believed it without question, and it was what Willow needed to know.

She nodded. 'I kind of knew that. Thanks for saying it.'

'Okay, so shall we get started? I'm not going to write anything down, but you can if you want.' Maybe that would give Willow a sense that she was in control of this.

'Yeah. I'd like to write it down.' She slid off the bed, a little more self-assured suddenly, and picked up a notepad and pen from her desk. Finding a blank page, she wrote her name at the top and two sentences underneath in capitals.

THIS HAPPENED TO ME. IT'S NOT MY FAULT.

Hope smiled. 'Good start. Shall we take a look at your clothes now?' She pointed to the jumbled pile on the floor at the end of the bed. 'Is this what you were wearing last night?'

It had been an hour and counting. Hope was obviously taking things at Willow's own pace and giving her a chance to talk, and that was just what Theo had wanted her to do. It was excruciating, though.

Phoebe had apologised for the mess in her room, which must be a reference to a couple of pencils that weren't quite straight on her desk, because Theo couldn't see anything else out of place. She'd fetched him a cup of tea, along with a sandwich that he'd been unable to even look at, and he'd remembered Hope's instruction and thanked Phoebe for looking after Willow, telling her that she'd done more than anyone could have asked.

That seemed to do the trick, and Phoebe gave him a smile. She told him about the arrangement that the girls had, if they went out together in the evening. They always came home in groups, leaving no one unaccounted for, and had alarms on their phones to alert their friends if they were in trouble.

'That's really useful.' Phoebe had showed him

the tracking app on her phone. 'Do your partners mind that everyone else knows exactly where you are?'

Phoebe gave him a startled look, as if he wasn't supposed to know about overnight stays with boyfriends. 'Not if they're worth our time, they don't.'

Theo chuckled. 'Good answer.'

There was an awkward silence, when he contemplated the sandwich and decided again that he couldn't eat anything. Then Theo asked Phoebe how her course was going.

'I'm doing orthopaedics at the moment. How is Hope doing with her fracture?'

This he could handle. 'It's a Weber A fracture. She fell down the stairs. What will you be looking for on the X-rays, and what's your advice on managing the injury…?'

Finally, Hope had tapped on the door and Phoebe had ushered her in, leaving them alone to go and sit with Willow. Hope handed him a sheet of paper, and Theo recognised Willow's handwriting.

'She took notes. She's asked me to show them to you. I think it's a bit easier for her than telling you face to face.'

Theo couldn't help smiling. 'So you figured out Willow's way of making sense of things.'

'Not really. I mentioned she could if she wanted to, and she seemed to like the idea.'

Theo nodded. 'Thanks for telling her this.' He pointed to the words at the top.

'Read, Theo.'

He took a breath, and scanned through the closely written words. No tears or damage to her clothing, no bruises or contusions. No signs of assault. He got as far as the urine test and the words began to blur in front of him.

'She can't spell benzodiazepines.' His hand was shaking now, and his heart thumped with a cocktail of emotions he wasn't quite ready to name.

Hope let the comment go, taking it for what it was, a desperate attempt to normalise the situation. 'She's asked me to take a blood test and we can find out which one.'

'Did she say…?' Theo stopped himself just in time. He knew that Hope would have promised Willow confidentiality, and if he wanted to know anything he had to ask his daughter.

'She asked me to tell you that any drug that's in her system isn't self-administered. If that's what you're wondering.'

He nodded. 'Thanks.'

'And she wants to report this to the police. I told her that it was her decision and no one was going to pressure her either way, but she was quite insistent about wanting to help stop this from happening to anyone else. She's a very brave young woman, Theo. You have a lot to be proud of in her.'

'We need to call them?'

'I did that, and Willow spoke to them briefly. I insisted they send someone here. I don't want her having to go down to the station. It may be an hour or so, but Willow's okay with waiting.'

'Hope, I can't thank you enough for this.' He felt tears on his cheek and brushed them away, impatiently, getting to his feet. 'I'm sorry. I should go and see her…'

Hope was on her feet too, barring his way. 'She's trying really hard to be strong, Theo. You know your own daughter best, but can I suggest that you might need to be stronger and let her know how you feel about this?'

He nodded. Hope was right. He'd hidden his emotions from Willow when her mother had left, knowing how frightened she was. They'd worked it out, but it had taken a while and several temper tantrums from Willow before Theo had realised that what she'd most needed was for him to be honest with her.

And right now, *he* had one overwhelming need. Hope seemed to know that too, and she wound her arms around his waist. He hugged her tight, suddenly able to breathe again. It was love in its purest form, and needed no explanations or justification.

When he drew back, he could see it in her eyes. It quietened his raging heart, allowing him to think more clearly and do what he needed to do.

'There's one more thing, Theo. I imagine Willow might want to come back to Hastings with you for a few days, and I think that might be a good idea. If you both want, then you can stay with me.'

'No, it's really good of you to offer, but…' Hope didn't have people back to the house. She had her own issues in that respect.

'It's okay. You've helped me come to terms with the hoard, and if Willow can accept it then I can too. There's plenty of room downstairs. She can have the spare bedroom and you could take the sofa bed in the sitting room. It's only five minutes from the surgery so you can pop in to see her for lunch if you want, and there's the garden if she wants to sit outside. She can borrow my car if she likes. I haven't used it for four weeks now so it could do with a drive around…'

And there was the kitchen. Hope wouldn't know this, but one of Willow's coping strategies was to cook.

'If you're sure? You might find yourself presented with a three-course dinner every evening. Willow's a good cook.'

'In that case, I'm going to have to insist.'

Suddenly his brain stopped turning. Theo wanted to do something, and couldn't think what. Maybe falling at Hope's feet and telling her that he wasn't sure how he'd lived this long without her.

'Off with you.' Clearly that wasn't on Hope's mind as a possible next move. 'Go and give your daughter that hug she's waiting for…'

CHAPTER NINE

IT WAS A long day. The young woman police officer, who arrived within the hour, was sensitive and kind, but had to admit that it was unlikely that the person who'd spiked Willow's drink would ever be found.

'We'll be reviewing CCTV footage and what you've told me helps us to build up an overall picture,' the police officer told her. 'It gives us a start with identifying areas of danger and preventing this kind of thing from happening again.'

Then there was a visit to the local sexual assault referral centre. Their tests confirmed Hope's findings, and that too didn't completely set Willow's mind at rest.

'What if they…touched me?'

Hope hesitated, but Theo knew how to answer that question. 'What do we know, sweetheart? You can't always stop people from doing things to hurt you. But you can decide how you're going to deal with it.'

Perhaps he'd said that to her when her mother left. Willow smiled suddenly and nodded.

He was a rock. One that allowed itself to have a tender heart. Theo waited patiently while Willow packed some things, and then gave her some time with Phoebe and the other young women in the house. Willow was slowly beginning to emerge from the shadow of last night, taking a peek at the sunshine of today.

The spare bedroom, which had once been Hope's mother's room, was light and sunny, with a coat of new paint on the walls. Here, Hope had been able to let go of the old bedding and specialist equipment, because she'd never felt it was a part of either of their lives, just a practical necessity. She put Willow's clothes into the wardrobe and chest of drawers, and then stopped for a moment to take a breath. *This* was what all the stress of clearing the house was for. Having somewhere that might shape the future, instead of living always in the past.

Willow had seen the spices in the rack in the kitchen and smiled when Theo asked her what she fancied for dinner.

'Your special tacos, Dad.' She turned to Hope. 'You'll love them.'

Hope *had* loved them, but she wasn't going to deprive Willow of the pleasure of seeing her love them all over again. And the momentary exchanged glance with Theo sent shivers down her spine. That could be their little secret.

Willow started to yawn before they'd finished eating, and went to bed early. Theo sat with her for a while and Hope heard them talking quietly together, before he joined her in the sitting room.

'Asleep?'

Theo nodded. 'Yeah. One minute she was talking to me about this term's course project and the next she was out like a light.'

'You want a drink?' Hope had been on her feet for much of the day, and she waved her hand towards the cabinet that held glasses and bottles, a little too achy to move.

'I'll have the other half of your tonic water, if you're not going to drink it.' He indicated the open bottle next to Hope's glass.

'Help yourself. It'll only go flat if you don't.'

He nodded, fetching himself a glass, and filling it, then sitting down next to her. 'How's your leg?'

'Oh…you know.'

'Yes, I do. That's why I asked.'

'It hurts a bit. It'll be better in the morning.'

He nodded. They were filling the silence, because that contained all of Theo's hopes and fears for Willow.

'How are *you* doing?'

Theo grimaced. 'Coming to terms with the idea that I could actually tear someone limb from limb. Is that a red flag for you?'

Hope shook her head. 'Only if you actually do it. It's perfectly understandable to think it. Maybe imagine me beating them with one of my crutches?'

'Okay. There's a boundary to aim for.'

He was tapping his foot, turning his glass in his hand. Theo never hesitated when something needed doing, but when there was nothing he could do, it got to him.

'You could take those boxes over to Eastbourne tomorrow, if you need some lifting to work off your frustration. I'll stay here with Willow.'

'I might just do that. They'll be at the library?'

'Yes, they said they would when I called to say we weren't going to be turning up today. You can take them any time.'

'Tomorrow would be good, if that's okay. Thank you. For everything…' He reached for her hand, curling his fingers around hers. An echo of this morning, when intimacy had seemed so uncomplicated.

'My pleasure.' Hope readjusted the thought. 'Not really pleasure… I wouldn't have wanted to be anywhere else, though.'

He lifted her hand to his lips, planting a soft kiss on the back of her fingers. Shards of a more compelling emotion began to pierce her heart, and Hope knew that she had to let it go.

'So what's Willow's term project all about?' She gave Theo's hand a squeeze, before reluctantly drawing back.

'Something you might be interested in. It's all about art and design as a way of ordinary people telling their stories.'

'How does that work?'

'I'm not entirely sure which direction she's taking with it. But she showed me some pictures of embroidery done in the early years of last century and pointed out the centrepieces. Purple and green...'

'Suffragette colours.' Hope smiled.

'You're ahead of me. I didn't see it at first. Once you knew, though, the designs made complete sense. Like statements of intent, hiding in plain sight.'

'That *is* interesting. Like my picture frames.' Hope nodded towards the two frames that had been professionally cleaned and polished, and were hanging in pride of place on her wall.

'Yes, exactly. You should show them to her. She'd be interested. If you don't mind her taking a few photographs, and maybe including them in her written submission.'

'No, of course not. I'd rather like that.' Hope thought for a moment. 'What's with the quilt that she was hanging onto? It took me a while to get her to let it go, so that I could check her for injuries, and I see she's brought it with her.'

Theo chuckled. 'That's made from pieces of fabric she picked up when we were in Kenya. That was during her year out, before we came back to England, and I was doing my thing while Willow got involved with a scheme for digging wells in rural villages. She started coming home with fabrics she'd bought, telling me that it was her way of supporting local economies, but it was a lot more than that to her. Then she cut the lot up, and made quilts out of it, one for her and one for me.'

'You still have yours?'

'Of course. I may travel light, but I keep the things that really matter. That was the year that Willow started to branch out, and do things her own way.'

An idea started to form at the back of Hope's mind. She wasn't sure how it might work, or whether it was even something she wanted. Maybe a good night's sleep would dismiss it as impractical.

'Will you sleep?' She stifled a yawn, indicating the pile of bedding stacked on the sofa-bed on the opposite side of the room.

'I'll be out like a light. Maybe wake up once every hour, listening for her.' Theo shrugged. 'It's a while since I've done that.'

'They do say that you never stop being a dad.'

'I'm hoping not. It's one of the best things that's happened to me so far, however many ups and downs there are to it. Why don't you turn in?' He nudged her gently.

'I think I might. I'll just sort out the duvet for you...'

'I can do that. Go and get some sleep.'

That wasn't a bad idea. Before she gave in to the feeling that she was becoming a part of Theo's life, and curled up with him on the sofa bed, there to comfort him if he woke. That would definitely be stepping over the boundaries she'd set. She had to let Theo face tonight alone. Anything else would be selfish. Hope slid to the edge of the sofa, concentrating on not looking back as she made her way slowly towards the door.

Theo *had* woken during the night. He'd listened for Willow, and a couple of times stood quietly behind her open door, listening to the sound of her breathing. Somehow he'd managed to stop himself from moving towards the door of Hope's bedroom. If she'd left it open, then he wasn't sure whether he'd be able to resist the temptation to wake her, just to spend a few moments of a lonely night with her.

But Hope was at a crossroads in her life. She had a chance to tackle some of the regrets that haunted her and Theo's part in it all was to accept that at some point he'd have to stand his ground, smiling as he waved her off to the new adventures that she could only experience alone.

But he could make the most of a new day. By the time Hope appeared in the kitchen, up and dressed, and then Willow, still wearing her pyjamas, he had several breakfast choices ready and waiting. Hope tucked into eggs and bacon, with toast, and Theo tried not to notice whether Willow was making inroads into the muesli and yoghurt she was toying with.

Hope waited until they'd all reached their second cup of coffee, and then swung into organisation mode. 'I'd love to hear a bit more about this project that your dad's been telling me about, Willow. It's a nice day—we could go and sit in the garden?'

Willow grinned. Hope had unerringly identified the thing that was keeping her going at the moment, and Theo felt the muscles that had obstinately refused to relax overnight begin to loosen.

'I haven't decided what to call it yet. I'm thinking *Ordinary Histories.*'

'Sounds fascinating. Are you still up for taking my little piece of ordinary history over to Eastbourne, Theo?'

'What's that?' Willow asked.

'It's not something that people have made for themselves,' Hope explained. 'Old newspapers, for a local history archive.'

'Oh. Yeah, I'm more interested in more personal voices. Expressed by making things,' Willow agreed, and the prospect of having to sort through ten boxes of newspapers a second time receded. Theo was happy to miss out on that. The first time had been difficult enough for Hope.

'I could. Unless there's something I can do here?'

Hope's raised eyebrow and Willow's pained expression told him there wasn't. 'Dad, you know you're no good at sitting around when you could be doing something useful.'

The most useful thing that he could do at the moment was something that made his daughter feel better. But Hope had that covered for the next few hours at least, and Theo couldn't deny that inactivity wasn't going to make *him* feel any better.

'You're sure?'

'Stop fussing, Dad.'

'Yes. Stop fussing, Theo.'

He chuckled. Theo knew his limitations, and taking both Willow *and* Hope on when they'd both decided on something was obviously unwise. 'Okay. You want me to get something for dinner, on the way back?'

Hope nodded, and Willow shot her a querying look. 'Would you mind if I cooked?'

'Feel free to cook as much as you like. The kitchen's all yours whenever you want it.' Hope grinned at her.

'Thanks. I'll give you a call, Dad, and tell you what to get…'

The trip over to Eastbourne had taken a bit longer than expected because Theo had stayed to help catalogue everything, knowing that Hope would appreciate a copy of the list. Then Willow had called, with her shopping list, and he'd had to visit several shops to get everything. Clearly she had a Kenyan curry in mind for a late lunch, this afternoon.

He knew that Hope would look after Willow, but still his heart began to beat a little faster as he parked at the front of the house and made his way round to the kitchen door. There was a rug, spread out on the grass in the back garden, with no one sitting on it. And in the kitchen, some of Willow's books and coursework were on the table, but no one was there, either. He dumped the shopping bags, wondering if Hope and Willow had decided to pop out.

'Anyone here?' he called, and heard the thump of sudden activity above his head.

'Up here…' Hope's voice drifted down the stairs.

Hope never let anyone upstairs—at least, only him. Theo climbed the stairs, reminding himself that he didn't begrudge Willow this gesture of trust.

He found them in the front bedroom. A space had been cleared around an old-fashioned, heavy wardrobe, and the contents had been sorted into piles on the floor. Willow had clearly been doing the fetching and carrying, while Hope sat in one of the two single seats contained in the S-shaped frame of a Victorian conversation seat.

'Hi, Dad.' Maybe Willow had worked out that this was his and Hope's secret place, because the look on her face was identical to the one that had greeted him when she was a teenager and he'd discovered her doing something she shouldn't.

'We've been having a good time, while you've been gone. I asked Willow to come and have a look at some of my mother's old dresses. She says she can make something for me, from all this.' Hope's firm tone indicated that if there was any blame attached to the enterprise, then it lay firmly with her.

'I suppose as long as you think this is having a good time…' Theo teased, and Willow rolled her eyes at him.

'Dad!' She grinned in Hope's direction. 'He doesn't understand about clothes.'

Fair comment. These things meant something to Hope, and Willow loved old styles and fabrics as well. It was probably best to move on, and get the full story from Hope later.

'I got all the shopping you wanted. I'll help Hope clear up here if you want to get started.'

Willow flung her arms around his neck suddenly, kissing his cheek. 'Thanks, Dad. Can we talk, later?'

'I'd really like that.' He gave his daughter a hug.

They heard Willow reach the bottom of the stairs, and Hope looked up at him thoughtfully. 'She's putting a brave face on it all. I told her that you were doing the same, and suggested that maybe you should talk to each other about that.'

'You never did do anything by halves, Hope.'

'You want me to?'

He shook his head. If he'd thought that Hope would give Willow anything other than good advice, he'd never have left them alone together today. If it was confronting, then so be it.

He walked over to her, sitting down in the empty half of the conversation seat. Each facing different ways, but when he leaned back they were almost face to face. It felt gorgeously intimate.

'Are you sure about this... Willow making something for you?'

'Which one of us don't you trust?' Hope's gaze met his.

'That's not an answer, I trust both of you. But you do know that when Willow makes things it almost inevitably involves scissors.'

'Yes, I know.' She was almost whispering, as if the piles of clothes might hear her.

'And you're happy with that. Willow taking a pair of scissors to your mother's dresses.' He nodded towards one of the piles. '*Your* dresses, from when you were little.'

'It'll be really good for her to have a project. Something to think about...'

Theo leaned towards her, his forearm resting on the padded rail between them. 'I appreciate the sentiment, and you're right. But I want to know how *you* feel about it.'

Hope lay her hand in the crook of his elbow. Each sensitive nerve screamed for more, although the architecture of the seat prevented it. Theo had never thought about furniture too much before but the magnification of each look, each gesture, was a triumph of desire over the manners of a bygone age.

'I knew all of this was here, my mum's wedding dress and my dad's suit. But I realise that I've never actually looked at any of it. Mum certainly didn't in the ten years I was living here. She knew that it was all stored up here and that seemed to be enough for her. When Willow took them out of the wardrobe, my dad's suit was full of moth holes, and all of the lace on my Mum's dress was gone as well.'

A tear formed in the corner of her eye and Hope blinked it away, smiling as he reached across to brush his fingers across the back of her hand.

'It's okay. It made me see that I can't preserve anything of my parents' lives together by locking it away and letting it slowly decay. It has to change to stay alive. So I'm going to let Willow make something of it all.'

'Willow's good with her hands, and she's got a talent for fabric. I'm not sure I could live with some of the things she comes up with, but they always have something about them.' But this was a bold step for Hope. 'As long as you're really sure.'

'Really sure is a bit much to ask, Theo. Don't you dare tell Willow that, because I've just spent half an hour convincing her that it's okay. But I want to do it, because I have to make these decisions if I'm ever going to be able to walk across any of these rooms without having to weave my way around boxes.'

'Okay. So when is she going to be starting this project?' Theo wondered if he might have a word with Willow and get her to take the dresses back

to Brighton, for this mystery project, so that Hope
didn't have to actually witness the first cut being
made.

'That's another thing. She needs a bit of help
with it, and she has a couple of friends who she
says are pretty good with a sewing machine. She
reckons Phoebe will be up for helping as well. I
imagine they'll need a bit of space so I suggested
she ask them over here. Willow said she wanted it
to be a surprise, so I said I'd go somewhere next
weekend and leave them to get on with it.' The
slight quirk of her lips told him that Hope wasn't
a hundred per cent comfortable with the idea.

'You're...?' Theo shook his head. 'Can't they
go to my place?'

'I suppose they could. But I've got more room,
and... I was thinking I might go away for the
weekend. Or if you wanted to stay here with them,
perhaps I could stay at yours? Just for the Saturday night. If you didn't mind, that is...' She took
her hand from his arm, breaking the connection
between them. As if she had no right to depend
on their friendship.

Theo sighed. 'How about this? Your ankle's not
really strong enough to drive yet, and if you stay
at mine you'll be at a loose end and sitting around
wondering what's happening here. I'll pick you up
on the Saturday and we'll drive in whatever direction the wind's blowing. Find a hotel for the night
and come back on the Sunday evening.'

Had he just asked her to go away with him for the weekend? Theo hadn't meant to, but it did sound suspiciously like it. Hope had the grace not to look quite as shocked as he felt at the idea.

'I haven't been away for the weekend in years.'

Hope had spent far too long looking out to sea and dreaming. It was time for her to start exploring a little. And Theo couldn't deny wanting to be a part of this first foray into the unknown.

'That's one good reason to go, isn't it?'

She thought for a moment, and then smiled. 'It's a really good reason to go. Let's do it, Theo.'

CHAPTER TEN

HOPE HAD BEEN waiting for something to go wrong. But things had gone smoothly at the medical centre, and there were no sudden emergencies that demanded their presence over the weekend. Willow had been slowly coming to terms with what had happened to her, and had spent the week filling a notebook with sketches and shopping for supplies, neither of which Hope enquired too closely about. Theo's car hadn't broken down, and neither of them had been struck down by a sudden, mystery illness.

She was up early, choosing a pair of wide-legged trousers that would accommodate the support boot, in case the wind was blowing in the direction of any long walks. Her favourite, colourful top made her feel ready for anything the weekend might throw at her. Theo arrived at eight o'clock, looking even more mind-numbingly gorgeous than usual, in a pair of pale chinos and an open-necked shirt.

'We're going to do this?' She walked out to his car to meet him.

'Looks like it. Are you still on board with it all?'

'Willow's already asked me this morning. It's a *yes*.'

Phoebe and two other friends arrived at eight-thirty, crammed into a car with several large boxes and a selection of bags. Hope's weekend case was already in the boot of Theo's car, and she waited as he said goodbye to Willow, giving her a hug.

'Which way is the wind blowing today?'

He grinned, jerking his thumb in a westerly direction. 'That way?'

Theo clearly had something planned. That was okay because being a doctor, or a caring daughter, generally implied that Hope was the one who applied forethought and planning to any given situation. Today there was none, and it felt deliciously adventurous.

'Sounds good.'

The morning was clean and crisp, with clear skies promising a warm day ahead of them. Theo was keeping to minor roads, avoiding the main coastal towns, and winding his way westwards through farmland and villages. They stopped for coffee in a pretty high street, parked for a while at the top of an ancient beacon to admire the view, and marvelled at wall paintings in a tiny thirteenth-century church. Today was all about the journey. Their destination would wait until they were ready.

By the early afternoon they'd reached Dorset, and Theo turned onto the motorway, grinning when he saw Hope's look of disappointment. 'We're a little behind schedule. We'll be there in half an hour.'

'So there *is* a schedule? And a *there*? I thought we might just be driving until we ran out of road.'

'And then building a boat?' He teased her. 'We only have two days. Keeping going until you run out of road is going to take a bit longer than that.'

All the same, their meandering pace had disconnected Hope from a world where time was everything and stopping to investigate whatever the horizon presented them with felt like a good thing. They left the motorway, driving down towards the coast, and Theo parked in a small car park, behind a pebble beach with a jetty running out to sea.

'I thought you said you weren't planning on running out of road?' Hope got out of the car, feeling the warm wind tug at her hair and clothes.

'We haven't. Not quite, anyway.' Theo pointed towards a string of rocky outcrops, which curved away from the beach. The larger one, right at the end, boasted a small cluster of stone clad buildings nestling amongst the trees.

'We're spending the night there?'

'We can. If you want to.' He grinned. 'Actually, I have reservations, but that doesn't sound so much like an adventure.'

'It is for me. Thank you, Theo.'

'My pleasure.' He looked at his watch. 'We have half an hour to wait. They bring a boat over every hour on the hour. There's a café over there that they recommend.' Theo nodded towards a brightly painted building a little further up the beach.

'Or there's the beach.'

He nodded. 'You want to look for fossils?' This stretch of coastline was known as the Jurassic Coast, because the steadily eroding cliffs contained thousands of fossils of creatures that once swam in the Jurassic seas.

'Only if they're within an arm's length. I'd like to just sit and watch the world go by.'

Theo decided to go in search of a cup of tea, and Hope watched as he strode along the beach. That was almost becoming a hobby, not so much because the back view was any better than the front, but because she'd never be able to look at him like that when he was walking towards her. A little forbidden pleasure went a long way, and she felt a tingle of appreciation at his broad shoulders and well-knit frame. The way he seemed so free, here, the wind tugging at his shirt and ruffling his hair.

He returned with the tea, and they sat for a while, looking out to sea. They'd come so far together since Theo had walked unexpectedly into Hope's consulting room, but it had taken this journey for Hope to be able to focus on what really mattered to her.

'Don't forget me, Theo. We're both going to be moving on, but...' Now that she'd said it, the admission that he meant more to her than just a friend seemed all too clear in her words.

He turned towards her suddenly. 'I never forgot you, Hope.'

Maybe she should leave it there. It was what she wanted to hear, even if Theo had looked away now, and was spinning stones from the beach, down towards the water line. The movement of his arm was becoming more and more forceful, until one, long throw propelled a stone into the sea.

'Stop, Theo.' Hope lay her hand on his arm. 'What's bugging you?'

He heaved a sigh. 'Did your heart ever break, Hope? For the first time.'

She nodded. Hope didn't dare say his name…

'Mine broke when you left.' Theo whispered the words so quietly she could hardly hear them over the crash of the waves.

'Mine too. When I knew I couldn't come back to you.'

They stared at each other. This was all Hope needed to hear.

'Then we both know why we shouldn't do it again.' Theo's fingers brushed her cheek and she smiled at him.

'Yes, we do.' She picked up a stone, throwing it towards the water. An incoming wave meant that at least it got a little wet when it hit the ground.

'Not bad.' Theo was weighing another stone in his hand, clearly intending that it should go further, even if it was bigger than the one that Hope had just thrown.

'What have you got there, Theo?' Hope stopped him from throwing the piece of striated grey limestone just in time. He looked at it more closely, and she saw a small, ribbed section of rock sticking out on one side. 'Is that an ammonite?'

'I think you're right. Hold on…' Theo got to his feet, jogging to the car, and came back with a small bag that contained a hammer with a chisel head and two pairs of safety glasses.

'You always keep these handy when you travel?'

'I had the advantage of knowing where we were heading. And your collection upstairs proves that you have a history of sorting through stones on the beach.' He handed her one of the pairs of safety glasses, and balanced the stone on its side, tapping it carefully with the chisel end of the hammer head.

Nothing happened. Perhaps this stone didn't want to give up whatever treasure lay at its core, and they should leave it be. Hope was about to suggest as much, when Theo found a weak point in the striations and a sharp blow opened up a split in the stone. He grinned, handing it to Hope, and she carefully prised the two pieces apart, gasping at the intricate patterns inside.

'Look, Theo, there are three of them.' One ammonite was almost an inch in diameter, and there were two other smaller ones, all perfectly preserved. 'Aren't they beautiful?'

He nodded. 'You'll take that home, won't you? It's something special.'

'Not all of it.' She handed him one half of the stone, and he shook his head.

'These belong together.'

'Half each. So our hearts don't break again.'

He smiled suddenly, closing his fingers around his half of the stone. 'Yes.'

They'd seen the boat setting off from the island, and by the time it arrived, Theo had collected their bags from the car, and they were ready and waiting on the jetty. The boat moored several feet away, and a tanned, middle-aged man strode towards them.

'Hi, I'm Tim Rutherford. Dr Lewis...' Tim shook Theo's hand vigorously. 'And Mrs Lewis?'

'Dr Ashdown,' Theo murmured and Hope wondered whether taking a step away from him might have eased the confusion. She let go of Theo's arm, deciding to climb into the boat on her own.

'Dr Ashdown. Apologies... Let me help you with your bags.' Tim bent to pick up their luggage, and saw the folding walking stick that lay across the top of Hope's weekend bag. This time he jumped to the right conclusion, grinning at her and holding out his hand to help her safely into the boat.

It was only a few minutes before they reached the island and were shown along a wooded path that led to the hotel. The reception area was light and airy, and as warm and informal as their welcome had been. Tim tapped the keyboard of a computer on the reception desk, extracting two key cards from a drawer and pressing them against a card reader.

'These are your keys. My partner Denny and I run this place, and if there's anything you need then we're here to help. There isn't a great deal to do here apart from eat and relax, but I trust you'll find both of these activities a very special pleasure.'

'I'm sure we will. It's beautiful here.' Hope looked up at Theo and he nodded, clearly pleased with his choice of destination.

They were shown through to the back of the building, and Tim opened two adjoining rooms, glancing around each of them to make sure that everything was in order. Then he indicated a bell-press by the door, which would summon a member of staff, and left them alone.

The rooms had a calm, modern-traditional feel and were decorated in muted shades of blue and cream. There were large, luxurious beds, timber furniture, and in Hope's room a large bay window made the most of the spectacular view, while Theo's had French doors that opened onto a balcony.

'This is beautiful, Theo. How ever did you find this place?'

'It was recommended by a friend I used to work with. She and her husband come here every year and unwind for a week. If I'd known it was this nice, I might have saved it until we could stay a little longer than just one night.'

This night was perfect, because it was the first one that Hope had spent away from home in a very long time. She'd wanted to remember it, and it was becoming increasingly obvious that it would be impossible to forget.

Hope loved looking out to sea. Just standing on the beach, taking a few deep breaths, always seemed to separate her from her troubles and doubts, and crossing the water to an island made them feel very far away. She could concentrate on a leisurely walk with Theo, taking his arm when the ground was a little too uneven for her. Then showering and changing, to meet him in the restaurant downstairs. They ate a superb meal, the muted sounds from the kitchen and bar drowned out by the crash of the waves outside the floor-to-ceiling windows.

It seemed so natural to go back to Theo's room together for coffee, opening the French doors and sitting on the small patio outside. The hotel was small and built for privacy, and there was no one but Hope to see Theo's smile of relaxed pleasure as he stretched his long legs out in front of him.

Sunset was a time for talking. Hope spoke about her father, how he knew so much about so many different things and how he could make anything seem full of magic. How her parents had met a little late in life, but had been made for each other. Theo responded with tales about the places that he and Willow had been, and the highs and lows that accompanied caring for a troubled teenager.

'It can't have been easy. But she's turned into an amazing young woman.'

Theo chuckled. 'Most of that is her doing, not mine. I just provided her with bed and board and watched her grow, and I wouldn't have missed that for the world. In case you hadn't noticed, I'm in the process of letting her go now.'

'Ah. Which is why you've practically been living at my place over the last week,' Hope teased him. 'Not that you weren't entirely welcome. And deeply needed.'

'That's different. She's an adult now, and she can make her own decisions. I get to listen and say what I think, without any expectation of her actually taking my well-thought-out advice.' He waved his hand, dismissing his own input. 'I still can't help wondering what she's doing now. If she's okay...'

Hope looked at her watch. She had the answer to that. 'Drinking and dancing, probably.'

'What?' Theo's head snapped around suddenly. 'Don't tell her I asked, but do you think she's really up to that right now?'

'It's okay, Theo, she's not making the rounds of the Hastings hotspots. I had a telephone conversation with Phoebe, and asked her to bring some music along with her, and she made a few suggestions about their favourite cocktail ingredients. I thought that they might like to party a little, just the four of them, but that Willow would need a safe space to do it in.'

The lines of worry in his face softened. 'That's really thoughtful of you. If they make any mess...'

'She's twenty years old, Theo. I assume she knows how to use a vacuum cleaner and get a few stains out of the carpet. They might be in the garden, anyway. There's nothing nicer than dancing in the dark on a night like this.'

'Yeah. Now you mention it...' His lips twitched into a smile. 'Would you mind holding that thought?'

'Happy to.'

Theo got to his feet, walking through the room and out into the corridor. Hope watched him go, then allowed herself a few moments to savour the thought of dancing in the dark. She heard the door open and close behind her and turned to see Theo, holding a bottle of champagne in an ice bucket.

'May I suggest a drink and a dance?'

'You may.' Hope walked into the room, where Theo had put the ice bucket onto the credenza and was bending to take two glasses from its shelves.

'And will you accept the offer?' He seemed keen to hear her say it.

'Yes. A drink and a dance would be very nice.'

He nodded, opening the champagne and pouring it. Everything else seemed to be slipping away, borne on the soft breeze that billowed in from the sea as Theo picked up the TV remote, switching to an easy-listening music station, which filled the room with the soft tempo of dance.

His gaze didn't leave her face as he handed her one of the glasses. His free arm wound around her waist and she felt the rhythm of his body against hers. Swaying together in the half-light, letting the exquisite feeling of having him close lead the way. Hope raised her glass, tipping it against his when he did the same.

'What should we drink to?' he asked.

The tenderness in his face, maybe. Or the way her body seemed to be melting against his, a perfect fit.

'Remember the last time we kissed, Theo?'

'Vividly.'

And then he'd broken her heart. And she'd broken his. The thought gave her courage to do things differently this time. 'I regret so many chances I've missed. The one I regret the most is the chance we missed together.'

They were locked in each other's arms. She could feel every line of his body, but it was impossible to tell what Theo was thinking.

'I'd love nothing more than to spend tonight with you, Hope. But we'd be foolish to promise each other anything more.'

'Then we won't. I still want this chance, Theo.'

He nodded. 'To tonight, then. And no regrets.'

'Tonight.' The clear tone of their glasses meeting sealed the promise. Hope took a sip of her champagne, moving against him in the slowest of slow dances.

He took her empty glass from her hand, putting it with his on the credenza, and suddenly he was all hers. Strong and steady, letting her dictate the pace. When she stood on her toes, reaching up to kiss him, he responded with an unhurried passion, which might just drive her mad with longing.

'I'm not going to break, Theo.' He'd always treated her as an equal, demanding just as much from her as he demanded from himself, but he obviously felt that now was the exception to that rule.

'I might.'

'Then take me with you when you do.' Hope kissed him again, allowing her lips to linger against his until she felt him tremble. She didn't have the experience he did, but she knew all she needed to know. Theo was an honest and caring man who was never afraid to challenge her, and that was what she wanted from him now.

She kissed him again and fire started to flicker between them. They'd always talked, and now, in the soft quiet of the night, their whispered words had a physical power that drove them both on. Turning in time to the music, savouring each moment.

He caught her hand, laying it on his chest, and

Hope slowly unbuttoned his shirt, allowing her fingers to explore his skin. 'You've been taking care of yourself.'

He smiled. 'Just keep the reassurances coming, eh? You're even more perfect than the day we first met.'

'Nice to know. Even if it's not quite the case...' She gasped as his gentle fingers skimmed her dress, then cupped her breast. When he pulled her close again, she could feel how much that turned him on.

'Let me hear that again.' There was an edge of demand in his tone, which sent thrills down her spine.

'You have to work for what you want, Theo.'

He smiled. Theo never turned away from a challenge and he was giving this his undivided attention. Trailing soft kisses across her cheek, searching for the most sensitive skin. One hand slid down her back, pulling her in tight. The other moved against her breast, and a sudden, urgent feeling of desire rose from the pit of her stomach.

Watching and listening, exploring. Finding out the little things that aroused him and letting Theo discover ways to arouse her was the most exquisite delight.

They were both so close to losing control. He turned her around, backing her against the wall. One hand on the fabric that covered her breast, still, his fingers finding that sweet spot of sensation. The other travelling downwards, gathering the skirts of her dress, until she felt his hand skim her thigh.

'Theo…' She gasped out his name, giving in to a rush of pleasure and longing. That wasn't enough for him, and he didn't stop until she let out a trembling sigh.

Suddenly a knock sounded at the door.

They both froze for a moment and Hope felt a tear run down her cheek. No… *Please*… Had Theo remembered to hang the *Do Not Disturb* sign on the door? Hope glanced towards it and saw it dangling from the handle on the inside of the room.

Theo laid one finger across her lips, and called out, his voice sounding strangely normal. 'Not now. Thank you.'

'Dr Lewis. Sorry to disturb, but we have an emergency…'

CHAPTER ELEVEN

IT SURPRISED THEO how quickly he could come down from a feeling of intense and overwhelming pleasure. He gestured to Hope to stay where she was, out of sight of the doorway, buttoning his shirt quickly before flipping the lock to open the door.

Tim was suitably contrite over disturbing them, but when he quickly explained that the cook had had an accident with a cooking knife and was unconscious and bleeding heavily, Theo dismissed his apologies.

'You were right to let me know. I'll come straight away.'

'I will too...' Hope called to him, and when Theo looked round, she'd flipped into professional mode as quickly as he had.

'Thanks, I really appreciate it.' Tim's face remained impassive, as if it were perfectly unremarkable to find Hope in Theo's room, and Theo sent a silent thank-you for his discretion.

'Do you need to collect your ankle support?' Hope's ankle was strong enough to bear the weight of normal activity, but Theo didn't want her to slip and fall, in what sounded like an emergency situation.

'That's not a bad idea. You go, and I'll be there in a minute.'

Tim was already on his way, and Theo had to jog to catch up with him. When he followed him through the restaurant and into the kitchen, he saw the reason for the rush.

A man, dressed in a chef's white jacket, was lying on the floor, with another man leaning over him, applying pressure to a towel folded over his leg. At a quick estimate, there was probably half a litre of blood soaking the towel and on the floor.

'Have you called an ambulance?' Theo asked Tim.

'No, I thought it was best to come and get you first.'

'That's fine—call now. Tell them exactly what you told me, and that there's a doctor in attendance but we need someone here as soon as possible.'

'Right. Will do.' Tim got his phone from his pocket, and Theo turned quickly to the other man.

'You're Denny?'

'Yep. I was right here but I couldn't stop him from pulling the knife out, and then… There was so much blood…'

'What you're doing now is exactly right. That's the knife?' Theo glanced at the bloodstained kitchen knife on the floor and it looked undamaged, so hopefully there was nothing left in the wound.

'Yes.'

'Okay, that's good.' Theo quickly checked that Denny had managed to staunch the bleeding and gave him a reassuring nod. 'Can you keep up the pressure for a minute more while I check his breathing?'

Denny was pale with shock, but he nodded. Theo reached into the medical kit that was open on the floor and pulled on a pair of gloves. He bent down to check the man's breathing and heard the characteristic sound of Hope's boot on the tiled floor, behind him.

'Oh!' Hope's steps had quickened, and Theo felt the brush of her skirt on his arm as she came to a halt next to him. She didn't interrupt, but he knew she must be making her own assessment of the situation.

'His airways are unobstructed and he seems to be breathing without any difficulty. Will you keep an eye on that and I'll help Denny.'

'Yes.' She laid her hand on his shoulder, steadying herself as she sank to the floor. Hope hadn't needed to ask whether she could touch him a few moments ago, but now her murmured 'Excuse me...' confirmed what he already knew. Their delicious intimacy might not survive this interruption.

There was no time to think about that now. Theo fetched another clean towel, laying it over the top of the one Denny was holding. He leaned in, applying pressure, and on his word Denny pulled his hands away.

'What happened?'

'He put the knife he was working with into his

pocket to go and wash his hands. He slipped on something and… He got up again, and I saw the knife sticking out of his leg. Before I could stop him, he'd pulled it out and it started to bleed. He took one look at the blood and fainted.' Denny shook his head. 'If I've told him once, I've told him a hundred times about carrying knives around in his pocket.'

Denny was beginning to disconnect from the trauma of the situation, and Theo needed to keep him on track for a while longer.

'You did all the right things, Denny. Can you tell me approximately where the knife was sticking out from his leg?'

'Right here.' Denny pointed to his own leg, indicating a spot where a wound might well damage the femoral artery.

'Okay, thanks. Go and wash your hands and take a couple of deep breaths. Then come back here. We may need your help.'

Denny returned his smile. 'Right. Gotcha.'

Theo kept up the pressure on the wound and heard Tim call out behind him. 'They're asking if we can get him across to the mainland by boat.'

'Tell them no,' Hope replied. 'It looks as if the femoral artery is damaged and he needs to be transported carefully. Is there anywhere on the island for the air ambulance to land?'

'Yes.'

'Okay, that's what we need. If there are any

problems, I'll speak to them.' She glanced across at Theo and he nodded. At least nothing had got in the way of their ability to second-guess each other in an emergency situation.

The man started to stir and Hope leaned over him. 'Welcome back. You're okay, but I need you to stay still.'

'It hurts… There was blood…'

'I know.' Hope laid her hand on the side of his face, blocking his view of the pool of blood that Theo was kneeling in. 'The doctor has to press hard to stop the bleeding. What's your name?'

'Sam.' Hope had neglected to mention that she was a doctor too, and maybe Sam had come to the conclusion that she must be an angel. Her approach was always pragmatic and Theo knew she'd go with whatever got him through this.

'Hello, Sam. Now, listen to me. I know this hurts, but we really do need you to stay still.' She waited until Sam nodded his assent. 'Did you bump your head when you fell?'

'I don't know…'

'Okay. Let me just feel the back of your head… That's fine. I'm going to look at your eyes now…' Hope reached for the medical bag and tugged a penlight from the elastic insert panel at the top. She carefully completed her examination and then beckoned Denny over.

'Keep talking to him, and let me know if he becomes drowsy or non-responsive,' she instructed quietly, then turned her smile onto Sam. 'Denny's going to look after you while we see to your wound. Okay?' She squeezed Sam's hand and somehow got a smile out of him before she scooted awkwardly around to Theo's side.

'We're going to need to dress this if we can.' Theo had been watching carefully and blood was now starting to show on the surface of the clean towel. 'Can you see if you can find the pressure point?'

Hope nodded, taking dressings and tape from the medical bag in readiness and then finding a pair of scissors to cut the waistband of Sam's trousers and then down as far as she could towards the wound, so they'd both be able to see what they were doing. She carefully positioned the heel of her hand over the spot where the femoral artery ran closest to the surface, at the top of Sam's leg, warned Denny that he'd need to keep Sam still now, and used her weight to push as hard as she could. Sam groaned in pain, and Hope ignored him, leaving Denny to grip his hand tightly.

'Have I got it?'

'Yeah, think so.' Theo cautiously decreased the pressure, only now feeling the sharp throb in his arms and shoulders from the effort of staunching the flow of blood from the cut. 'Can you keep it up? I'm going to try to dress the wound.'

'Yes.'

They both knew that would be hard work for

Hope, particularly as she couldn't rely on as much body weight as Theo could. There was no need to discuss that right now. Theo carefully removed the towels and, as soon as he'd satisfied himself that the bleeding was temporarily stopped, began to work as fast as he could.

The wound was small, but very deep. Theo cleaned it quickly, and then packed it, binding each layer of dressings tightly. Then he bandaged the wound, holding a clean towel ready.

'Done.'

Hope nodded, releasing her pressure on the artery slowly. Theo watched for any signs of blood and saw none. 'I think we're good. I'll maintain compression, just in case.'

'Hear that, Sam?' After their concentrated effort, there was time to reassure Sam now, and she turned to him, smiling. 'Everything's fine, we just have to wait for the ambulance…' She turned to Tim, who had ended his call to the emergency services, giving him a querying look.

'The air ambulance should be here in five minutes. I'm just going to switch the lights on in the wildflower meadow.' Tim hurried away.

'You have a helipad disguised as a wildflower meadow?' She turned to Denny, the slight twitch of her mouth telling Theo just what she was imagining. An island with hidden mechanics below ground, which would roll the meadow back to reveal a fully equipped launch pad.

'It's a flat space with some landing lights. We had to provide access to the hotel for the emergency services, but it's never been used.' Denny didn't get the joke, but Hope flashed Theo an amused look. It was her way of dispelling the tension that hung over the small group, and he felt the muscles in his jaw begin to relax a little.

'Well, it'll be useful now. They'll be able to get you to hospital in double-quick time, Sam.'

'My wife… Will you call her?' Sam asked Hope.

'Yes, of course. Denny and Tim have her number?' Denny nodded. 'We'll her know that you're safe and on your way to the hospital.'

'Tell her… Tell her not to come.' Sam was pale and clearly weakened by shock and loss of blood, but he reached for Hope. This was important to him. 'Don't tell her I fainted.'

Hope smiled, taking his hand. 'No, we won't. Although I don't blame you for fainting. I probably would have done the same.'

'She has to stay home and look after the baby. There'll be no one to take her at this time of night.'

'I see. You have a little girl? How old?'

'Three months.'

'Ah. They're so beautiful at that age. I'm sure you'll be well enough to see her very soon, Sam.'

This wasn't just idle conversation. Hope was calming Sam, getting him ready for the flight ahead of him. If he was relaxed, maybe thinking of his wife and daughter, then he'd be able to face whatever came next.

Theo heard the low beat of a helicopter, circling and then coming in to land. Then Tim ushered the air ambulance crew into the kitchen, calling over his shoulder that several of the guests were asking what was happening, and that he'd be in Reception if anyone needed him.

The two paramedics brought blood and plasma with them, and a transfusion was set up immediately. The dressing on Sam's leg seemed to have stopped the bleeding temporarily, and the specialised gauze in the bleed control kit wasn't needed, but Theo felt more confident now that it was available, if the wound did start to bleed again.

'Going in five minutes. We can take a passenger.' One of the paramedics looked up at Hope.

'I'll go with him, thanks.' She answered immediately, turning as Theo cleared his throat softly. 'What, Theo? You're covered in blood and so is Denny.'

When he looked down, it came almost as a surprise to find that his pale chinos were dark with blood now. And Denny's shirt wasn't much better. Somehow Hope had managed to carry out a demanding medical procedure and only get two inconspicuous smudges on her dress.

'But how are you going to get back here?'

'That's no problem,' Denny interjected. 'You have your phone with you?'

'Yes, it's in my bag.' Hope gestured to her handbag, which was lying on a worktop near the door. She must have thought to grab it when she went to her room to fetch the support boot. 'Theo has the number.'

'Okay, I'll call Sam's wife and then text you my number. Call me when you're ready to leave the hospital.' Denny reached into his pocket. 'Here's some cash for a taxi. I'll bring the boat over and be waiting for you in the car park.'

'Perfect. Text me the number for Sam's wife as well so I can call her with an update...' She looked round as Sam was lifted gently onto the basket stretcher, and prepared for the journey. The ambulance crew wouldn't wait, but she made the time to shoot Theo a brilliant smile. 'Got to go. See you later, partner.'

A shaft of pure longing embedded itself deep in his heart. They *were* still partners, working together with the same synchronicity they'd always had. He watched as Denny produced a jacket with the hotel's logo printed on it, and wrapped it around Hope's shoulders. Then she was gone.

Denny broke the silence. 'Will he be all right? He has a wife and baby...'

The question that everyone needed to ask, and which no doctor could answer with one hundred per cent certainty. 'They'll be doing scans when he gets to the hospital and Hope will be able to tell us more then. But from what I saw, he has a very good chance of being up and around soon.'

'Thanks. And thank you for all you did.' Denny's face was still troubled. 'I don't think Sam would have made it without your prompt intervention.'

The minutes that Denny had been here alone, trying to save Sam and waiting desperately for help, must have seemed like hours. Hope would have gone in for a hug at this point, but Theo's style generally involved a little gentle logic.

'It's frightening how fast someone can bleed out from a wound like that. If you hadn't acted quickly and applied pressure to stop the bleeding, Sam could have died before I even got to him. You saved his life, and all of the chances he has now are there because of what you and Tim did.'

Denny nodded. 'Thanks, I really appreciate your saying that. Why don't you go and take a shower, and I'll send someone up with whatever you want from the bar? Or some tea if you prefer?'

Sitting alone, waiting for Hope, didn't appeal right now. 'Or I could give you a hand clearing up here. We may as well do it now.' He indicated his bloodstained trousers.

'Absolutely not, Theo. You're done here. I'll deal with that.' Denny dismissed the suggestion.

'To be honest, I'd welcome something to do. I'll be waiting up for Hope anyway, and she'll be at least an hour or so.' Their moments together had gone now, and Theo suspected that they wouldn't be able to recreate them. The least he could do, though, was to be there when she returned, to re-affirm their friendship. That had been lost once, and Theo prided himself on learning from his mistakes.

Denny shook his head. 'I suppose…if you absolutely must…'

He'd helped clean the kitchen floor, then showered and changed his clothes. Theo had then wandered back to the reception area, in search of something else to do, and Tim had intercepted him and insisted on ordering tea and keeping him company.

After two hours, Denny appeared, saying that Hope had called to let him know she was on her way, and he would take the boat across to the jetty and wait for her. He returned fifteen minutes later, Hope leaning on his arm as they walked, and then Tim and Denny disappeared, leaving them alone.

'You waited up.' She smiled up at him.

'Nah. Just happened to bump into you, by chance.'

'Thank you for bumping into me, then.'

Theo offered her his arm, and she took it. 'Is your leg hurting you?'

'It aches, but the boot protected it really well. I'm really glad I went. The scans showed that there was just a small nick in Sam's femoral artery, and they took him straight into surgery to repair it. I spoke to the surgeon afterwards, then called his wife, and I think I was able to put her mind at rest. She'll be going to see him first thing tomorrow, and I expect he'll be awake and recovering by then.'

'That's a good end to the evening, then.' Not the one he'd wanted, but they both understood that sudden interruptions went with the territory. Theo stopped outside the door to his room, pressing the key card against the reader. If Hope wanted to say goodnight now, then he had to let her go, but that didn't mean he couldn't suggest an alternative.

'Would you like something to drink? I've been making good use of my time while you've been gone, and have permission to use the staff drinks cupboard for tonight.'

'Nice going. So I have a choice between instant coffee and a crumpled teabag?'

Theo chuckled. 'Tim and Denny do things a lot better than that. There are at least a dozen different strengths of coffee, various different teas including herbal. Cocoa, hot chocolate…' He let the idea of hot chocolate sink in a little.

'Do you think hot chocolate would be too much?'

'No. Sit down and I'll go and get it.'

'Take your phone and get pictures of the cupboard, as well. I may have to accidentally leave them around on Rosie's desk,' Hope called after him.

When he returned with the hot chocolate, she'd

168 THE GP'S SEASIDE REUNION

taken off her boot and propped her leg up on a couple of cushions. Her ankle looked a little swollen but she was wiggling her toes with obvious pleasure as he set the mug down beside her.

She took a sip, smiling at him. 'You haven't lost your edge, Theo.'

'Neither have you.' Theo sat down opposite her. 'We were pretty good together once upon a time.'

'You make it sound like a hundred years ago. We still are.'

Theo turned his attention to his drink for a moment. Maybe that would give him time to think, but he suspected that no amount of thinking would change the conclusion he'd already come to. The one that all of Hope's body language was telegraphing.

Now was the time to just say it. To bring closure to what might have been, and save what they actually had. 'I think... The moment for champagne is gone.'

Hope twisted her mouth in a gratifying expression of remorse. 'Yes. This sounds really crazy but... It's one thing to allow the night to carry you away, and quite another to *decide* on it.'

'It's not crazy. I feel that way too.' If they spent the night together now, that would be a thought-out commitment. Something that could be broken. 'I don't regret knowing that you wanted to, though.'

Hope smiled suddenly. 'Me neither. We never understood that about each other before.'

But even that wasn't going to change their minds. There was nothing more to say now, but they could sit together, keeping each other company as the sound of the sea drifted in through the still-open French doors. Hope didn't seem disposed to move yet, and maybe she wanted the reassurance of his company, as much as he did hers.

'So what's next on your to-do list?' Late at night, with the moon rising clear in the sky, those kinds of questions came more naturally than in the heat of the day.

Hope thought for a moment. 'I reckon… A few more weekends away. Without the stabbing part, of course.'

'Naturally.' Theo decided not to ask whether that included him. Maybe Hope wanted to go alone.

'And a party. I'd like to have a party when the house is a bit clearer.'

'Sounds good.' A party was much more likely to involve him.

'What about yours?'

Theo considered all of the things he *might* want and then settled on one concrete object that he really did want. 'I'd like a table. A big, sturdy one, that's gathered a few bumps and scratches over the years. One that I can fill, for Sunday lunch.'

Hope chuckled. 'You haven't had a table before?'

'Yeah, loads of them. And Willow and I have filled them up on plenty of occasions. I never did have a table of my own, though.'

'I get that. I like the table I have in my kitchen. I probably have a couple more upstairs you could have, but that's not the point, is it? It's got to be bought especially for you.'

'Yeah. I'll be seeing whether you'd like to help me choose it, when I have a room large enough to put it in.'

Hope smiled. 'Yes, I'll definitely do that.' She suppressed a yawn. 'I think it's time I went to bed. I'll dream of weekends and parties, and you can dream of tables.'

That didn't seem much of a trade for having Hope by his side. Curling up together, and dreaming only of her. But none of this was about things, it was about giving each other the space to grow. He got to his feet, picking up their cups and putting them onto the credenza, next to the bottle of champagne. He could carry them back down to the kitchen later.

Hope was on her feet too, the cushions back in their place, and the support boot tucked under her arm.

'Goodnight.' She smiled up at him.

'Goodnight, sweetheart. Sleep well…'

CHAPTER TWELVE

HOPE HAD WANTED to wake early on Sunday morning. Make the most of the island and take a walk, maybe. Then have a leisurely breakfast with Theo, in the open-air seating area outside the restaurant.

But going to bed alone had allowed her thoughts to wander, to places they shouldn't. How would it have been if she and Theo had fallen into his bed, together? What if they'd changed all of their plans, and by some twist of fate it had all worked out?

She knew the answer to the first question. The echoes of what they *had* done were still thrumming through her, convincing her that what they might have done would have pushed all the boundaries of marvellous. The second question was more difficult and she lay awake for some time, trying to find an answer that didn't involve catastrophe.

The first light before dawn was filtering into the room before she finally got to sleep and Hope woke late. She showered and dressed quickly, finding Theo in the very same spot she'd reckoned on having breakfast with him. He was sitting alone, an empty coffee cup in front of him, reading the Sunday paper.

'Sorry...' She sat down opposite him. 'Why didn't you wake me?'

'I've only just got up myself. I reckoned on

doing the crossword over a second cup of coffee before I gave you a wake-up call.'

Or he could have knocked on her door. After last night, maybe that was a step too far. 'That's okay, then. I feel a bit better about oversleeping. You want a hand with the crossword?'

He smiled, handing over the paper. 'I'll take wild guesses and you can write down the right answers.' He looked up at the waitress, who'd seen Hope arrive and come to take their order. 'May we have another pot of coffee, please? And…?'

'Croissants for me,' Hope added.

'Croissants for two, then. And I don't suppose you have a spare pen, do you?'

The waitress nodded, taking a pen with the name of the hotel inscribed on it from the pocket of her apron and handing it to Hope. 'I heard about Sam. Thank you for all you did. He's a good guy. Great cook as well.'

'It was our pleasure.' Theo smiled up at her. 'Have you heard how he is this morning?'

'Yes, Tim said that his wife called. I don't really know the details but he's going to be fine. That's what matters, eh?'

'Yeah. It is,' Theo agreed. 'We'll be shifting for ourselves at lunchtime, I guess?'

'No, Tim and Denny worked all of the menus out with Sam, and they're stepping in.' The young woman leaned forward conspiratorially. 'They'll be fine with entrées and the first course—they often help out if we're busy. Between you and me, I'm not so sure about the desserts.'

'Good to know. Thanks.' Hope smiled at the waitress and she turned away, leaving them to the crossword.

Everything between her and Theo was just as it had been. When they'd finished the crossword, he divided the paper in half, and they sat in the sun together, swapping pages as they read them. They took a walk down to the beach that Tim had recommended yesterday, to look for fossils, but this time they found nothing. Lunch was marvellous, and when Hope took a risk on the chocolate mousse, it tasted delicious.

But something was missing. The easy friendship, the jokes and the pleasure in each other's company—they were all still there. But the frisson of excitement, wondering what was behind the warmth in Theo's eyes—that was gone. They packed their bags and exchanged hugs and handshakes with Tim and Denny before one of the other staff took them back over to the mainland. As they got into Theo's car, it was clear that the wind had changed, and was blowing them back home.

'Look at this.' Tim had handed Theo a sealed envelope as they'd left, telling him to open it later, and he'd torn it open before starting to drive.

'Oh! Two vouchers for a weekend break at the hotel. That's so kind of them.'

'Yes, it is. Have you still got Denny's number in your phone?'

'Yes, I'll call him when we get onto the road and thank him. You keep them both safe.' Hope handed the vouchers back to Theo, wondering whether Willow might like a spot of fossil hunting. The hotel was wonderful, but she'd left memories of what might have been behind her there. She wasn't sure she wanted to go back again.

Their route home was less meandering than the one they'd taken yesterday, and Theo stayed on the motorway for most of the way. Then, unexpectedly, he drove straight past her house.

'What's going on?' Hope turned in her seat, wondering if Theo had caught sight of something she hadn't.

He turned the next corner and came to a halt. 'It's ten to six.'

'That's okay, isn't it? Willow said about six.'

Theo laughed dryly. 'Yeah. When Willow says about six, she means that she'll be racing around in a complete frenzy until exactly six o'clock. Being ready for something early just isn't in her repertoire.'

'Ah. We'll wait, then, I wouldn't want to cramp her style.' Hope folded her hands in her lap, staring ahead of her. She'd forgotten all about what Willow and her friends might be getting up to this weekend, but now they were home…

'Nervous?'

'Terrified.'

Theo nodded. 'Me too. It'll be okay, though. I have a lot of confidence in Willow. She won't let you down.'

'I have a lot of confidence in her too. It's *me* I'm worried about. Suppose I find that I've promised more than I can deal with, Theo? That she's done something wonderful and I can't bear to look at it?'

Theo reached out, brushing the back of her hand with his fingertips. One of those simple gestures that they'd thought nothing of before, but this was the first time he'd touched her since… Since every caress had provoked fire.

'I have *every* confidence in you, Hope. You've taken your time and thought about what you want to do. I think you've made some great decisions about how to repurpose things in a constructive way.'

'Thanks. You make me sound almost well adjusted at times…' She grinned at him, reaching out to take his hand. Theo flinched momentarily and then smiled back, winding his fingers around hers. He felt the awkwardness too.

But they were putting it behind them, and moving on. After a laughing countdown to six o'clock, Theo turned in the road and parked his car behind Phoebe's in Hope's driveway. He followed Hope around to the back of the house, and they saw Willow rush to the kitchen door, flinging it open. 'Dad! I said six o'clock!'

Theo gave her an amiable smile, ignoring the sounds of frenzied activity coming from somewhere at the front of the house. 'It *is* six o'clock, sweetheart.'

'Well…couldn't you be fashionably late, for once?'

Probably not. Theo needed to have a good reason to be late for anything. Hope stepped in, giving Willow a hug. 'Did you have a good weekend?'

She felt Willow's exasperation melt away as she hugged her back. 'We had a great time, thank you so much. We danced on your lawn in the dark, like wood nymphs.'

'Sounds fabulous. We'll just go and sit in the garden, until you're ready, shall we?'

Theo nodded, and Willow jumped as Phoebe burst into the kitchen. 'Hi, Dr Lewis. Hope, thank you so much, we've had a wonderful weekend.'

Willow shot Phoebe a querying glance and Phoebe nodded. Willow ushered them inside, taking Hope's hand to lead her towards the sitting room. Phoebe followed, making polite conversation with Theo.

Their friends, Jo and Alice, were standing by the fireplace. Willow turned Hope around to face the sofa and she gasped.

'Do you like it?' Willow whispered, agitatedly.

'I…' She was speechless. But she had to say *something* because everyone seemed to be holding their breath. 'It's beautiful, Willow. Give me a minute to take it all in…' Hope fanned her face, looking at the quilt that covered the sofa.

There were two central panels, each with a different appliqué picture. A couple standing in front of a church, a family at the seaside… But they were personal, something just for her. The little girl wore a blue patterned dress made from the fabric of one that Hope had worn as a child. The couple at the church were fashioned from material from her father's suit, and her mother's wedding dress.

Around the pictures, there were entwined strips of fabric from clothes that had been worn and discarded, but were now brought back to life. And the deep borders of the quilt featured patchwork squares and diamonds, arranged by colour to give a shaded, rippling effect.

'I love it. I *really* love it. How did you do all this in just two days?'

Willow beamed at her. 'I had it all planned out and I did the templates for the appliqué during the week while you were at work. Then I cut and placed everything, while Jo and Alice sewed. And Phoebe made the book—did you see that?'

'Because I'm no good with a sewing machine.' Phoebe picked up an album, hidden under the quilt, and shyly gave it to Hope. Inside were photographs of each of the items of clothing that had been used, some on hangers, and some arranged carefully on the floor, with folds at the elbows and knees that made them seem almost alive. Phoebe had used different backdrops, tiled and wooden floors, along with the white walls of the spare bedroom and the exposed brickwork in the kitchen.

'You're brilliant with a camera. This looks like a fashion shoot. And it's a lovely memento of what it all looked like before it became a quilt.'

'It's documentation, really.' Phoebe was clearly pleased with Hope's reaction.

'Way to go, Phoebe.' Theo was craning over, looking at the pictures. 'A good doctor documents everything.'

Hope laughed. 'He hasn't mentioned that before by any chance, has he?'

'Of course I have,' Theo retorted, shooting Phoebe a conspiratorial look.

Alice brought out a cake and some sparkling orange juice from the kitchen, and Hope made sure to thank everyone individually.

'You're sure it's okay if we use pictures of the quilt in our end-of-term project?' Jo asked her.

'Of course. Willow asked me and I'd be really pleased if you did. You've all put a lot of thought and work into this. You'll take the rest of the fabric as well, I hope. Willow said that you could use it.'

'If that's okay… We had an idea that we might make a quilt about healing. You know, what happened to Willow and how making the quilt helped her.' Jo grinned. 'It's kind of circular. A quilt telling the story of a quilt.'

'That's really interesting. I'd love to see it…'

The room was alive with chatter, and Hope noticed that Theo was circulating too, making sure to speak with everyone. Finally he made his way back to her.

'What do you think?'

'I think this is…just more and better than I could ever have imagined. It doesn't feel like letting go of things, it's like regaining them. It's so impressive that they did all of this in such a short time.'

Theo nodded. 'They're smart young women. Unfortunately even their organisational flair isn't going to fit four people, two sewing machines and goodness only knows how many boxes of fabric into Phoebe's car.'

'Now you mention it…' Hope frowned. 'They could leave the fabric here if they wanted, I suppose. Collect it later.'

'And you're going to be able to resist sorting through it all again?'

Hope knew what she'd find, and she was okay with the idea that the clothes had been cut into pieces. That didn't mean she actually wanted to see them in that state. 'It's a bit like having an operation. You're really happy about the results but you don't necessarily want to see the blood and gore.'

He chuckled. 'Only you, Hope. Steady as a rock when it comes to blood and gore, but liable to faint clean away over some fabric. But since that's the case, I'll take Willow and the boxes back to Brighton, and Phoebe can take Jo and Alice, along with the rest of their things.'

'No, Theo! You've already driven a long way today. Leave it here. I'll put it upstairs, lock the door and you can hide the key.'

His eyes softened suddenly. 'How else am I going to say goodbye?'

She hadn't thought about that. Waving everyone off, and then finding herself alone with Theo. Feeling the warmth of a beautiful gift, and the excitement of his smile. They'd made their decision, and it was the right thing for both of them, but that didn't mean she couldn't be tempted.

'Theo, I don't regret one moment of this weekend. But you're probably right.'

He chuckled. 'Yeah, I think I probably am. I'll go and have a word with Willow, before she decides that she, Jo and Alice are going to have to take the train back to Brighton.'

When Hope had waved them all off and closed the front door behind her, the house seemed suddenly very still and quiet. Willow and her friends had left everything clean and tidy, and there was nothing to do, apart from soaking her dress in cold water to get the spots of blood out. Then she was alone amongst the memories.

She walked into the sitting room, moving the quilt aside a little to sit down on the sofa. Each piece of it held a fragment of the past. The texture of a dress with a shirred bodice that she'd had when she was little, secured with tiny stitches and preserved. Tiny seashells and stones on the beach, made from the sequins on one of her mother's old tops, which shimmered in the light. A piece of one of her father's shirts from the eighties. Crying a little seemed okay, because they were happy memories that were no longer locked away upstairs.

But Theo...? She was so desperate to keep his friendship, it had made her ruthless in cutting away things that might spoil it. It was a hard road, and both of them were fighting to allow the other to reach a place where they could find peace with the past.

Tomorrow would be another day. The memory of what they couldn't have would fade, and Hope would begin to focus on what *was* possible. She slipped off her sandals, curling up on the sofa, under the warm comfort of the quilt.

CHAPTER THIRTEEN

SOMETHING HAD BROKEN between them. Hope seemed just the same, and Theo imagined he did too, but he knew it wasn't his imagination. The jokes between them seemed more brittle, more needy of the other's smile. Touching her was no longer a careless warmth and coffee was something he drank alone.

It would mend. It *had* to mend, because nothing else could justify the decision they'd taken. Then, suddenly, it did. On Friday afternoon, Hope walked into his consulting room without bothering to knock, put a mug of coffee down in front of him and plumped herself down in the chair on the other side of his desk.

'Are you thirsty? Or just hiding out from someone, before afternoon surgery begins?' Theo smiled at his own joke, and didn't care that Hope wrinkled her nose in reply, because her green eyes were warm and alive.

'Neither. The coffee's to give me a kick-start for the afternoon, and I've been talking to Sara Jamieson about something that might interest you.'

He could identify with the need for a kick-start. Hope had been looking tired this week, and he'd had difficulty sleeping as well.

'Okay.' He picked up the mug, taking a sip of his drink. 'What on earth…?'

'Is that mine? I used the emergency rocket-fuel capsule, and put some sugar in it.' She tasted hers and nodded. 'Yes, this one's yours.'

Theo didn't feel a trace of embarrassment about swapping cups. They were definitely back on track and all he needed to find out now was what had prompted the rocket-fuel coffee and Hope's change of heart.

'What's up? You could have given yourself heart palpitations in your own office.'

Hope smirked at him. 'It's really not that bad. It tastes pretty strong, so you just think it's waking you up. Sara Jamieson passed me a letter that I thought you might be interested in. It's from a drugs charity…' She slid the piece of paper she was holding across his desk.

'Yeah, I've heard of them. They do a lot of good work.' Theo started to scan the letter, but Hope clearly wasn't in a mood to wait while he read it.

'They're setting up a scheme for general practices, initially in the South-East, but if it's a success they want to go countrywide. They say that GPs are often the first line of support for drugs patients, and often we don't have the support or the knowledge to be able to give them what they need. I thought of you.'

So that was what had brought about this change. He and Hope had never had any hesitation in calling each other out on things, and that was what she was doing now.

'Sara mentioned something of the sort to me, although she didn't say that there had been a letter. I told her that I thought it would be better if someone else represented the practice.'

'Yes, she told me. What were you thinking, Theo?'

It was a fair question, even if Sara Jamieson had neglected to ask it. He was well qualified to help the practice out with this.

'I was thinking exactly what I said to Sara, that I'm only here on a temporary basis and that liaison over a valuable, ongoing project such as this is much better done by one of the permanent staff. Such as you. And...' Theo shrugged. He didn't need to tell Hope what had happened to him.

'And that you burned out.' Her tone held all of the warmth and understanding that Theo knew Hope was capable of.

'Yes. Although I didn't mention it. I'm not going back, Hope.'

She pursed her lips. 'That's not what I'm asking you to do. I've already told Sara that I want to be involved, so you wouldn't be letting anyone down if you dropped out. But this might be an opportunity for you to revisit a medical field that was a big part of your life. Gain a little perspective, and perhaps some closure, which will allow you to go forward with more certainty.'

There was no disagreeing with Hope sometimes. She knew that he was proud of the difference he'd been able to make for Amy and her family, and that Theo had begun to wonder whether he'd thrown the good things about his previous job away with the bad. 'I'm not making any commitments, but if I *did* decide to get involved…?'

'Second page of the letter. Selected practices have been invited to a one-day informal meeting, to exchange ideas and identify areas of need. We could be a part of making this work, Theo…'

He held up his hand, and Hope fell silent. 'You know you can squeeze a *yes* out of me, but I need to think about this. If I do go then I want to give it a hundred per cent.'

She nodded. 'It didn't occur to me that you wouldn't. It's not an easy decision, and it's yours to make.'

'And the meeting is…' He flipped the letter over. 'Tomorrow week?'

'Yes, the letter took a week to get here, and then Sara had it on her desk for a few days. I'm going to get back to them straight away and say that the practice would like to be a part of this, and that I'll be attending. They need final numbers by next Wednesday, so you'll have to let me know by then if you want to be involved.'

It had taken a difference of opinion to break the ice and carry them back to where they wanted to be. But then most of their disagreements were born out of concern for each other, not about pulling in different directions.

'Okay, thanks. I'll let you know as soon as I decide.'

'Great. Do you want another gulp of my coffee before you start your afternoon surgery?'

Theo chuckled. 'Are you trying to poison me?'

'Not right now, you probably have a full list of patients for this afternoon. Maybe later...'

Theo had turned the idea over in his head, and slept on it. Hope was right, this did feel like going forward, rather than going back. He picked up his phone, writing a text to let her know what he'd decided and then deleting it. Since when had he texted Hope, when it was possible to call?

She sounded as if she'd slept in this morning, but she woke up as soon as he told her that he'd be joining her next weekend.

'That's great. You can give me a lift up there.'

He smiled. Hope would always turn things around, pretend that he was doing her a favour by coming along, when she was the one who'd done him a favour by challenging his doubts.

'I'm going over to Brighton tomorrow, to see Willow for lunch. Jo and Alice are busy but Phoebe's probably going to join us. Want to come?'

There was a pause. Maybe he'd assumed a little too much.

'Yes, that would be nice. What time?'

* * *

The room was only half full. Looking around, Hope couldn't see anyone from the other general practices in Hastings, and the staff of the South London charity who'd welcomed them here were glancing nervously at their watches.

'Do you think everyone's turned up?' she murmured quietly to Theo.

'From the number of coffee cups and pastries over there, I'd say no.' He nodded towards the refreshments table. 'Perhaps there's a hold-up somewhere on the Tube and they'll all come flooding in a bit later.'

'Hope so. I was looking at the display boards and they've done a lot of work on this...' She turned as a man of around fifty, with close-cropped grey hair, hurried up to them.

'Theo! As I live and breathe. What are you doing here?' The two men shook hands warmly.

'I could say the same. Willow and I are both based on the south coast now. She's at university and I'm working as a GP.' Theo turned to Hope. 'This is my colleague, Dr Hope Ashdown. Hope, this is Dr Ted Magnusson. He's a psychiatrist specialising in the treatment of addiction. I've been trying not to bump into him for the last fifteen years now, and he turns up in the most surprising places.'

Ted shook Hope's hand. 'Nice to meet you, and

don't listen to a word that Theo says about me. Which practice are you from?'

'Arrow Lane in Hastings.' She saw Ted suppress a smile. 'Probably the worst-named medical centre since 1066.'

Ted laughed, and Theo shook his head, chuckling. 'This is your project, Ted?'

'Not really, we're looking to recruit someone to lead it, and it's not been easy to find the right person. I've been the head of Community Outreach here for a couple of years and just taken a step up to CEO, so I'm babysitting today.'

Theo nodded. 'And how's Jenny?'

'Still running rings around me, without even breaking a sweat. Actually she is breaking a little bit of a sweat at the moment. We're about to become grandparents, and she's more nervous for Jess than she was when all three of ours were born.'

'Congratulations.' Theo shot Ted a delighted smile. 'When's the baby due?'

'Yesterday. I'm rather hoping I'm not going to get a call today…' He looked quickly around the room. 'We thought we'd have more people coming. Perhaps it wasn't such a good idea to have it on a Saturday.'

'The practice couldn't have spared both of us during the week,' Hope observed, and Ted nodded.

'That's exactly what we were thinking. But GPs are under a lot of pressure and I think that a project like this sounds like just one more thing to have to take on board. It's really not. It's intended to make their lives easier.'

'I'm all for that.' Hope smiled at him. 'I've got a few questions, for the Q & A, later.'

'Marvellous. The more the merrier. I think if we can start a discussion then people will start to see the potential of the project a bit more clearly. You know your own patients best, and you have a key part to play in co-ordinating services, but sometimes it's difficult to know where to start.'

'I can identify with that. Theo's been steering me in the right direction with one of my patients recently.'

'You had access to the best. We'll be more than happy if we can reach the giddy heights of second best.' Ted laughed as Theo shook his head. 'Look, I'd better go and circulate. Catch you later…'

Theo watched Ted go, and then turned to Hope. 'Don't listen to him. Ted was my team leader when I started out, and he taught me everything I needed to know, and then a bit more for good measure. What do you say we get the ball rolling with some hard questioning? He'll appreciate something to get his teeth into…'

When everyone had been ushered to the lines of seats, for a short presentation followed by questions and discussion, Theo made a beeline for the back row. Hope followed, realising that the strategy was intended to include everyone in the to and fro of questions and answers.

Ted's presentation was met with obvious interest, and a low hum of conversation between the other delegates. But when he asked for questions, silence settled on the room.

'Ladies first...' Theo nudged her to her feet and she saw heads swinging round to follow Ted's gaze.

'I'd like to ask—you talked about a knowledge base and person-to-person advice, which doctors can access. What form do you expect those resources to take, and how could I integrate them into a busy working day?'

'Thanks. That's the crucial question. How can we add to your effectiveness, rather than simply burdening you with another layer of administrative effort?' Several people in the audience nodded their heads. 'We're very open to your comments on this one, because you know what you need better than anyone. But we envisage it working like this...'

By the time Ted had finished answering, his audience was hanging on his every word. Theo waited a moment in case anyone else wanted to ask a question and then got to his feet.

'I have a foot in both camps. I worked for many years in drug-related fields, and I'm now working as a GP.' Hope had wondered whether he was going to come clean about that, and from everyone's reaction he'd done the right thing in making his position clear. 'How are you going to reconcile the different approaches of various different drugs agencies?'

Ted's smile broadened. 'I thought you might want to know about that.' His gaze swept the audience. 'Theo and I have worked together before, and he's touching on an issue that we've both faced. Let me explain…'

The question opened out into a wide-ranging discussion, which involved several other members of the audience. Theo was enjoying this. Hope had always known he'd have something positive to give to the day, but he seemed inspired, as if the young man who wanted to change the world had just resurfaced in him. She'd encouraged him to come here, and it suddenly felt as if it was a first step towards losing him.

The Q & A session ran for longer than expected, and by the time it was finished the room was buzzing with conversation. Ted held up his hands for silence.

'Thanks, everyone, for a great session. I've learned a lot. I'm going to hand you over to my colleague Ahmed, who'll be leading the afternoon session, where we'll be listening to what you want and need from an information service. But first, there's a buffet lunch waiting next door, and please do feel free to enjoy the sunshine in our roof garden, which is through the doors on the right.'

There was a burst of applause, and Ted hurried over to Theo and Hope. 'Guys, you really got things moving. I can't thank you enough. I'm really sorry but I have to go...'

'Jess?' Theo asked.

'Yep, Jenny texted me fifteen minutes ago and they were just leaving for the hospital.'

'What are you doing still here? Give them both my love, and if you get a moment, let me know how everything goes.'

'Of course, leave your number with Ahmed and I'll text you. Thanks, Theo. And you too, Hope, it was such a pleasure—'

'Go!' Hope laughingly commanded him. 'Before anyone catches up with you to ask any more questions...'

'Good day?' Hope took his arm as they strolled together in the evening sunshine, towards the car park.

'Yeah, really good day. You were right, when you persuaded me to come.'

'How right? One hundred per cent? Two hundred...' Hope bit her tongue. Why spoil this good day?

Theo shot her a querying look. 'What do you mean?'

Suddenly she wanted to be anywhere but here. Anything but right. 'You're not done with this kind of work, are you? It still excites you.' Her words sounded more like an accusation than anything.

He didn't answer straight away. That was answer enough. 'I find that I have something to give. But it was just one day.'

'You can't deny it, Theo, you have a lot to give. People who have fresh ideas and the ability to make them work don't grow on trees.'

'Making ideas work takes time, and I have other commitments at the moment. Today was great and seeing Ted again was a real pleasure. But it's not enough to throw over everything I've worked for in the last year.'

They'd reached Theo's car now, and his phone beeped. He leaned against the driver's door, taking his phone from his pocket, his movements sharp and cross. Then all of a sudden his face was wreathed in smiles. 'Look.'

He turned the phone around, and suddenly Hope had to smile, too. A newborn baby, its little face wrinkled in an expression of pure outrage.

'Ooh! Poor little mite.' Every instinct was commanding Hope to hold the baby in her arms and comfort it. 'Don't worry, darling. There's a beautiful world out there, waiting for you.'

Theo chuckled, turning the screen back towards him to read the accompanying text. 'It's a girl, eight pounds two ounces, and mother and baby are both well. No name yet.' His phone beeped again. 'Ah, look. I think she heard you.'

The little girl had clearly come to terms with her situation, and seemed to be dozing peacefully. Then another photograph arrived, this time of the baby with a serious, wide-eyed look on her face.

'If I know Ted at all, she already has him wrapped around her little finger.' Theo started to type a return text.

'Are you sending love? Send some from me, too. She's beautiful.'

Theo nodded. Ted's little granddaughter had done one of her first good deeds in the world, and lifted the mood between them. Hope had so wanted Theo to find his place in the world, and didn't much like herself for allowing her own feelings of rejection to get in the way.

'You want to come round to mine for something to eat?' She held out an olive branch and Theo grinned, stretching out his hand. Hope took a step towards him and he enveloped her in a one-armed hug.

'I'd love to. But I told Willow I'd give Phoebe a call tonight. Willow says she's starting in Thingy-atrics next week and she's got a few questions. She won't be around tomorrow when I go over to Brighton.'

'I know a thing or two about Thingy-atrics. You could bring your laptop over and I'll shout a few well-chosen words, while I cook something.'

'Since you're the expert, you speak to Phoebe. I'll cook.'

'We'll both speak to her. Then we can both cook.' Hope didn't know how she was going to let go of Theo, but they'd made their decisions and it was inevitable he would be moving on at some point. This friendship was far too precious to spoil, and if she was going to let him go, then she had to do it well.

CHAPTER FOURTEEN

THEO WOULDN'T HAVE blamed Hope for reacting badly to Ted's latest email. He had his own reservations about giving up the chance to see Hope every day, even if he knew that it would be coming to an end soon. Each moment of it had become precious.

But they'd already decided which promises to make to each other. Their commitment was to be friends, rather than lovers, and he'd promised that he would find a way to move forward and build a settled life. It was time to put those promises into action.

He walked into her consulting room at lunchtime on Wednesday, and she smiled up at him as he put the cardboard beaker down in front of her.

'Is that what I think it is?' She stripped off the lid and took a sip. 'Ah. That's nice. You can stay.'

In Hope's ever-changing world of favourite cafés and beverages, it seemed that caramel cream cappuccino hadn't been knocked off the top of her list yet. Theo probably spent far too much time noticing the trends, but the information could be useful at times like this.

'I've received an email. From Ted.'

She looked up at the two pieces of paper in his hand. 'Two pages? Sounds interesting.'

'He wants to set up a meeting. This is not an

offer, but he's wondering if I want to explore pos-sibilities.' He handed the job description over, and Hope focussed on it.

'Hmm. Head of Community Outreach—that's Ted's old job, isn't it?'

'Yes, they've decided to promote Ahmed and have him lead the project we were talking about on Saturday. He's got a lot of potential but not much experience, so he'll need some extra guidance.'

'And you'd be heading that up.' Hope looked up at him. 'But you said you weren't interested in going back to work with addiction-related issues full time?'

That was fair enough, he'd shut that conversa-tion down once. 'I've thought about it, and…it's still something I really care about. In my last job, the travelling didn't give me a chance to build up a solid support framework, which is what everyone needs when they're dealing with difficult casel-oads. It's something I'd want to discuss in depth, but I think this job will be different.'

Hope nodded, and then went back to the letter. 'Limited travel in the UK, not more than two days a month… Based in their London office, but after an initial settling-in period there's the possibility of working from home one or two days a week…' She looked up at him. 'Is this basically a PR job?'

Theo smiled. 'That's another thing I'd want to discuss. I don't imagine so, because Ted knows I wouldn't be interested in something like that and wouldn't even bother offering it.'

Hope nodded, smiling as she finished reading the letter. 'That's nice. The last paragraph. Ted obviously thinks a lot of you.'

'I think a lot of him. If I didn't know him and feel that he'll give the charity strong and imaginative leadership, I'm not sure how much serious consideration I would have given this letter. But as it is…'

'You're considering it.' Hope had the grace not to even hint at an I-told-you-so.

'What do you think?' If Hope asked him to stay, even if it was just on the basis of seeing where that led them, he'd write back to Ted this afternoon and tell him that he was in no position to take him up on his offer. He could find another job in Hastings, after this one came to an end.

'I think that you should at least talk to Ted about it. That can't hurt, can it?'

Somehow it did, though. Theo took a sip of his drink to conceal his dismay.

'I guess not. Ted suggested in the covering email that I go over to his place on Sunday, to meet the chairman of the board of trustees and several of the other executive committee members. Jenny will do one of her famous buffet lunches, and Jess will be there with her husband and the baby. We'll retire to his study for coffee and talk business.'

'He wants you, doesn't he? Softening you up

with lunch and a baby…' Hope flashed him an amused look.

'That's very much Ted's style. But yes. I've got to admit that the baby's his secret weapon. Only Sunday may be a problem…'

'Because that's your day for lunch with Willow.' Hope had a habit of seeing straight through him. 'Why don't I ask her over to mine? And Phoebe as well, or anyone else that Willow would like to bring. It'll be nice. Bit of girl-talk.'

'Am I ready for girl-talk between you and my daughter?'

'I'd say so. I know these Sunday lunches are your way of keeping an eye on her without crowding her, and I'd be disappointed in Willow if she doesn't know it too. This can be your weekend to back off a little, and receive a full report afterwards. In writing if you desire.' Her green eyes flashed with humour.

When Hope was in this mood, the one and only thing he desired was her. But he'd asked her what she thought, and she'd told him. Going back to question her again sounded as if he hadn't believed her the first time.

'Thank you. I'll give Ted a call now, and tell him I'm interested in talking some more about this.'

'Good.' She shot him an impish smile. 'Do I get a favour in return?'

'Anything you like.'

'Careful what you let yourself in for, Theo. Mrs

Perkins is coming in this afternoon, and she's struggling with the exercises the physiotherapist has given her. I wouldn't mind a second opinion, and she could probably do with a bit of encouragement from two doctors, instead of just one.'

Theo grinned. 'You underestimate yourself. But I'll be happy to see her if you think I can add anything useful.' He picked up his coffee, getting to his feet. He should listen to the advice that he would almost certainly give Mrs Perkins, and accept that Hope was right about most things.

It had been a nice day. Willow and Phoebe had turned up with home-made tiramisu, which Willow had balanced on her lap in a cool bag all the way from Brighton. They'd cooked and eaten and then gone to sit in the sun-filled lounge, where the quilt still commanded pride of place on the sofa.

Willow had hugged Hope before they left. 'Thanks for a lovely afternoon. I hope Dad didn't make you feel that you had to take over from him, while he's away at this mysterious work thing up in London.'

'I was the one who elbowed him out. I wanted to see you.' Hope shot Willow a conspiratorial look. 'Are you telling me that you feel a bit crowded?'

'No, not at all. I love that he's always there for me. I was worried that I was crowding the two of *you*. He told me about the hotel vouchers you were given and it would be nice for you to go away for a break.'

Was Willow trying to play Cupid? Hope ignored the thought. 'Have you mentioned this to him? That you'll be okay if you don't see him every weekend?'

'Not in so many words. I told him that the counselling from the university service is helping a lot and that I feel better.' Willow grimaced. 'Not completely better, but better than I did…'

'Recovering,' Hope suggested.

'Yes, that's it.'

'Your dad knows that there are things you need to do on your own, and things that he can help with. Just tell him.'

Willow thought for a moment. 'Could you tell him? He listens to you.'

Hope ignored that, too. She'd tried to conceal her feelings about what was happening over this new job of Theo's because she was the one person he really didn't need to listen to.

'He has to hear it from you as well. We'll both tell him, eh?'

'You've got a deal.' Willow grinned at her. 'See you later, then.'

'Soon, I hope.'

'Yes. Soon…'

Hope was sitting in the garden when Theo arrived, trying not to look as if she was waiting for him. He was carrying an armful of bound documents, and she didn't need to ask whether the day had gone well. Before he even got close enough for her to see the excitement in his eyes, she could tell his mood from the way he moved.

'Interesting day?'

He nodded, sinking into the empty deck chair next to hers. 'Very. How was yours?'

'It was really nice. Willow has something to tell you.'

He narrowed his eyes. 'Is she going to bail out on me next Sunday?'

'I think she's ready to. Do you mind?'

'No, I'm glad to hear it. As long as she's happy with that.'

Hope nodded. 'She seems to be. She told me she was feeling better about things, although not completely better.'

'Recovering.' Theo echoed Hope's assessment of the situation and she smiled.

'That's it. She wanted me to mention it, and I said I would but only on condition she told you herself.'

'Thanks.' Theo sighed. 'I've talked with so many young people in crisis, and I've learned to know when it's time to back off. It's so much more difficult to gauge when it's your own child.'

'I imagine so. Is it just me, or does Willow never say goodbye to anyone? Always "See you later".'

Theo chuckled. 'It's partly you. Willow doesn't

say goodbye to people who mean something to her. At first it was to do with her mother leaving, but I think it's just something she says now, as a way of telling people she values them.'

'That's nice. Listen to her, Theo. She knows you'll always be there when she needs you.'

He nodded, catching her gaze. Those silent gestures had always spoken more loudly than words, and Hope was going to miss them.

'So tell me all about *your* day. You want something to drink, I have plenty of juice in the kitchen. Cold chicken and home-made tiramisu leftovers.'

'Sounds nice. I've got a lot to think about…' He tapped his finger on the pile of bound documents that he'd dumped on the grass next to his chair.

'I'm not reading all that, Theo. I'll never get to work tomorrow. Give me the edited highlights.'

He chuckled as he followed her into the kitchen, putting the documents down on the table. Hope added the leftovers from lunch and two glasses, and sat down.

'So… I'm going to assume that no one's turned anyone down yet.'

Theo shook his head. 'We talked for quite a while, and they offered me the job. I have a week to think about it, and if I say yes they'd like me to start as soon as possible. They realise that I might not be able to.'

This was all going much faster than Hope had

thought. She poured herself some juice, swallowing down the lump in her throat.

'And your thoughts?'

'My initial concern was whether I wanted to go back into working in the charity sector, dealing with substance abuse. I explained exactly why I left in the first place. I thought it was important to be up front about that. The emphasis of this job is different, though—my day-to-day dealings will be with other medical professionals, along with many different kinds of agencies and employers.'

'And the part about whether you'll be using your medical skills?'

'Absolutely. Ted's very clear about that. The charity was actually founded by a group of six doctors who wanted to take an evidence-based approach to addiction issues, and fund research, as well as running clinics. The last CEO was keen to move away from that, but in promoting Ted the trustees have made a decision to return to their original remit. He's encouraging qualified staff members to spend an afternoon a week at their London clinic and take on their own cases. Doctors don't just deal with a client's substance-abuse issues, they have a holistic approach and support them in all of their medical needs if necessary. I said that was something I'd be very interested in doing.'

Hope nodded. 'Okay, I'm getting the idea that

this is something you feel you can commit yourself to. I imagine you'd have to move to London.'

He twisted his mouth in an expression of regret and she looked away. Seeing London as a problem would only eat away at Hope's resolve to think about what was best for Theo.

'One of their staff is going up to Scotland for a year, to help set up a network in Glasgow. He's renting out his house in South Norwood, and Ted suggested I speak to him if I wanted to move in closer to the office. This is going to be a demanding job, and coming down here at weekends would be easier than commuting up to London every day.'

Weekends. The thought made Hope tremble. Theo would clearly be coming to see Willow, but in a whole weekend he'd have time to see her as well. She swallowed down the idea, trying to think clearly.

'Then it all comes down to whether this is what you want. Is it?'

Theo rubbed his hand across his face, seeming suddenly at a loss. 'That's the question I don't know how to answer. What do you think?'

Hope thought the same as she always had: that she didn't want to lose Theo. 'It sounds like something that you *could* commit yourself to. Only you know whether it is.'

'But…' He reached across the table, taking her hands in his. 'I don't need to take this job. If you asked me to stay, I would.'

Suddenly, nothing else mattered. All that she could see were the new possibilities that flooded her world, leaving no room for anything else.

'This isn't fair, Theo. It's your decision and I can't make it for you.' Maybe he had a plan that he wasn't telling her about. Had Theo found a way to confound the inevitable?

If you asked me to stay, I would.

The words were tearing at her heart as Theo raised her fingers to his lips. This intimacy, never far from the surface, was so easy to fall into. So natural. Fighting it was so hard.

'Hope, I'm not asking for promises. I know you have your own life, and I have mine, and that our plans are very different. But there's something between us that just feels so right. We have unfinished business, and if you'd like me to stay until we've worked it out, then I will.'

'You mean…you and me? Together?'

'I mean that I'll keep the flat on, so that we can see as much or as little of each other as we like. Give ourselves time to see where that leads, and wherever it *does* lead then at least we'll both know that it was our decision, and we didn't allow circumstances to part us.'

'It's not even a matter of wanting different things, Theo. We have different pathways to follow if we're ever going to be the people that we need to be. I won't be the one that stops you from finding the healing you need.'

He shook his head. 'I'd never stop you either, Hope. But how can we really know that things wouldn't work out if we don't give them a try? We've both spent our lives juggling different priorities—we know how to do that, don't we?'

Theo's dark eyes were so tender. And he believed what he was saying. That she could venture out into the world, and he could find a home. That he could give up a job opportunity like this, without the sacrifice eating away at him.

That she would be able to bear his disappointment if she couldn't give him children. That loss and regret wouldn't sour their future together, and tear them apart. Some things could be changed and compromised on. Others couldn't.

'Theo, I'm sorry. I can't see how we can be together without hurting each other. I want you to go.' She didn't want him to go at all, but she wouldn't give him hope when there was none. She couldn't give herself hope.

A shadow fell over his face. Would this be the way she'd remember him? When all she really wanted right now was to see his eyes shining with warmth and humour.

He nodded. 'Then there's no more to be said. You've always spoken your mind, Hope, and I may not like it but I do appreciate it.'

He gathered up the bundle of bound documents. Hope watched as he walked to the kitchen door, willing him to look back and tell her she was wrong, but she knew he couldn't. He pulled the door closed behind him and she heard his footsteps on the path that led around the side of the house as he walked away.

Theo was gone. She hadn't even said goodbye because she couldn't bear the finality of it. And 'See you later' was far too big a lie.

CHAPTER FIFTEEN

TIME HAD SLIPPED through her fingers, spilling at her feet like a shattered dream. Hope had arrived at work early on Monday morning, because there was no point in staying in bed if she wasn't going to sleep. She'd got through the day, promising herself that tomorrow was time enough to figure out what she might say to Theo when the time came for him to leave. Something that was both regretful but conveyed her fond hopes for the future, maybe. Empty words that couldn't express her feeling of loss.

On Tuesday she felt a little more equal to the ordeal that loomed ahead of her. A constant stream of patients in the morning gave her no time for lunch, and in the afternoon she had home visits to make. She made it back to Arrow Lane at half past six, wondering if Theo would still be there, and she'd have the opportunity to speak with him.

Sara Jamieson intercepted her at the top of the stairs, beckoning her into her consulting room, and waving her towards the seat on the other side of her desk.

'Theo's made a list of outstanding issues. I'll be passing most of them over to Anna Singh in the morning, but there are a few that need your attention.'

Wait… Time finally stood still for a moment.

'He's gone already?'

Sara looked up at her in surprise. 'Didn't he tell you?'

'Um…yes, I knew that Theo had another job offer.'

'Yes, it all worked out very well. Couldn't have been better, in fact. I spoke to Anna just last week and she told me that she was seriously considering coming back to work early, because her husband's been made redundant. When Theo came to tell me about his new job on Monday, I called Anna and she said she was keen to come back right away. Her husband's been looking around, but things are very tight in his line of work so it makes sense for him to look after the baby for the next few months, while she works. And Theo's new employers wanted him to take up his new role as soon as possible. It sounds like a really exciting opportunity, doesn't it?'

'Yes. Yes, it is.' Hope was on autopilot now, numbed by shock. 'I didn't realise it would all happen so soon.'

'I expect he means to call you. Since you were out this afternoon, when he said his goodbyes.' Sara paused, looking at Hope intently.

'Of course. Or I'll call him. I dare say we'll have lunch before he leaves.' It was surprisingly easy to smile. When you could feel nothing, it was just a movement of the lips.

'I hope he keeps in touch. Although of course

we're already involved with the project run by the organisation he's joining, so we'll be seeing him again, no doubt. Anna said she'd be interested in being copied in on what you're doing there.'

'I'll go through it all with her when she's settled back in. She's welcome to attend the next session in a couple of months' time. It would be good if she's involved too.' A glimmer of feeling was tugging away at her heart, and Hope needed to cut this conversation short before it started to grow and overwhelm her. 'What's on Theo's list?'

'Ah, yes.' Sara handed over a typed sheet. 'He's up to date on everything, but there are a few outstanding test results, and he's listed those out in case they fall through any cracks. And, of course, Amy Wheeler. I see from Theo's notes she's doing very well.'

'Yes, she seems to be. She's attending all of her therapy sessions and she and her parents are keeping up a dialogue. It's early days yet, but the last time I spoke with Theo about her, he was very optimistic.'

'Ah, good. Theo's jotted down a few things you might want to look at in the future and…well, I suppose we can always refer back to him with any concerns.'

Or maybe Anna would, if Hope could persuade her. She stood, before Sara could think of anything else she wanted to say. 'I have a few things to do before I go, so if that's everything…'

'Yes, I'd better get on myself. I have evening appointments to attend to. Thanks, Hope.' Sara smiled, pressing the intercom to summon her next patient.

Her legs felt like lead, and even walking was an effort. Hope reached the safety of her consulting room and dumped her bag down next to her desk. Tomorrow would be soon enough to take her laptop out and transfer the patient notes she'd made onto the system. Right now she had to get home before she fell to pieces.

She counted the steps, down the stairs and out to the car park. Took a couple of deep breaths, before she started her car and drove home. The back door was too far to walk and as soon as the front door closed behind her, Hope sank to the floor and finally gave way to tears.

Theo couldn't shake the guilt. The one thing he'd thought about on the drive back from Ted's home was that this job offer was going to change everything. And he couldn't take it up without asking Hope, one last time, if this was what she really wanted.

And he'd lied. To himself and then to her. He'd pretended that there was a chance they could reconcile all the different things they wanted from life. Theo had tried to clip her wings, when he should have allowed her to fly away.

But he'd asked his question and she'd given him

her answer. And when everything had happened with unexpected speed, he'd left without a word. Because there was nothing he could say to Hope that would make things any better.

He'd moved from Hastings to London on the Wednesday and Thursday, then gone into the office to meet Ted for an orientation day on Friday. The weekend had been spent reading up on policy and procedures, and Theo had started work on the following Monday. For the last month he'd done little but work, eat and sometimes sleep. Trying to forget Hope and knowing that he never would.

'Two days.' Ted walked into his office, sitting down on the sofa in the corner. That was an obvious invitation for Theo to leave his desk and join him.

'Is that a challenge, or an observation?'

'Bit of both.'

Theo leaned back in his seat, smiling. Ted had a habit of opening a conversation in broad terms and allowing someone's reply to shape the direction it took.

'Don't let me stop you from getting to the point, Ted.'

'Since you're not going to talk about it, I suppose I'll have to. You've been working twelve-hour days, and had two days off in the last month. And you only took those two Sundays to see Willow.'

'I'm getting to grips with a new job, Ted. That all takes time.'

'Don't.' Ted frowned at him. 'You know what I think about that—this work is demanding and a work/life balance is everything if you're going to stay the course. You used to understand this. You've always worked hard but you made time for other things as well.'

Theo sighed. There wasn't any point in denying it, because Ted was far too canny for that. 'Yeah. You're right.'

Ted waited, and Theo resisted the impulse to explain.

'I'm right? Is that all you're going to say? Tell me something I didn't know already.'

'I'm not one of your patients, Ted.'

'No, you're not. My responsibility is much broader than that because you're my friend and you also happen to be an employee of the organisation that I head.' Ted grinned. 'For my sins.'

Theo held up his hands. 'Okay. As a friend, will you answer me one question?'

'Sure. Fire away.'

'You've been married for thirty years, and I know that Jenny has her own career and aspirations. That she doesn't always make the same life choices as you.'

'Thirty-two, actually. And yes, of course that's the case. I think that's why we've made it this far, and why we're planning on making it for another thirty-two years.'

Theo smiled. 'What do you do if things are leading you in one direction and her in another?'

Ted thought for a moment. He'd never give a glib answer when there was a more helpful one to be had.

'This is about you and Hope.'

'Is it that obvious?'

'Afraid so. I've known you for a while now, and it didn't take much expertise in body language to come to that conclusion.'

Good to know. It was actually *very* good to know that he wasn't the only person who thought that he and Hope were made for each other and that Ted had seen what Theo had considered the one, ultimate truth. The one he'd been hiding from for the last month.

'I'll rephrase, then. If Hope has one set of aspirations, and I have another, conflicting set, how do we even think about making a relationship? It's nothing to do with my having taken this job. It runs a lot deeper than that.'

'It's a tough one. I'm not sure that there's one definitive answer but... When Jenny and I found ourselves in that situation, we both sat down and thought about what was important to us personally. Just one thing. Whatever it was we couldn't do without.'

'And that worked?'

'It did for us. Made things a great deal simpler,

and we each knew what the other couldn't compromise on. Does that help?'

Maybe. Theo would have to think about it. 'Yeah. It's something to consider.'

'Anything else?'

'No. Thanks, Ted.'

Ted rolled his eyes. 'You win. Only…since I'm the boss around here I get to win sometimes as well. Not quite as often as you might think, but this is important. You're going to slow down a bit. At least take your weekends off, and going home at a reasonable time would be good too.'

'I hear you.'

'Are you going to do anything about it?' Ted clearly wasn't going to let go of this without some kind of assurance.

'Yeah. Actually, I am.'

Hope was just wondering where Willow and Phoebe had got to when she saw them walking towards the kitchen door, talking to each other intently. She opened the door, and Willow bounded forward, flinging her arms around her.

'I'm so glad to see you! You didn't mind me calling, did you?'

'Of course not.' Hope had already decided that there would be no embarrassed elephants lurking in the corner of the room. 'Your dad moving away doesn't mean we can't keep in touch, does it?'

'No, it doesn't.' Phoebe shot Willow an I-told-you-so look. 'Break-ups are always difficult when there's a child involved.'

Willow's eyebrows shot up. 'What child? You don't mean *me*, do you?'

Hope decided that shooing the elephants away was going to be more difficult than she'd thought. 'Sit down, both of you. I've made a cake.' Hope went to fetch the carrot cake she'd made, which was the latest in a series of experiments, and put it down onto the table next to the knife and plates.

Willow examined the cake carefully. 'Looks nice. You've been baking?'

Yes, actually. In the four weeks since she'd seen Theo, Hope had cried a great deal and baked. She had to admit that there was something to be said for baking, but it hadn't yet mended a broken heart.

'Cut a piece, and see what it's like on the inside. You'll have coffee?'

'Tea for me, please,' Phoebe asked, watching as Willow carefully cut a slice of cake. 'The cake looks fine in the middle.'

Willow broke off a piece. 'Tastes good, as well.'

'Help yourselves, then.' Hope brought the coffee and Phoebe's tea over to the table and sat down. 'And tell me what you've both been up to.'

'I've finished in Paediatrics, and I'm in A & E now. It's really hard, but I love it.'

Hope nodded. 'It's been a long time since I worked in A & E, but if I can help with anything give me a call. Have you decided on what you want to specialise in yet?'

'If I do well on this rotation, maybe Emergency Medicine.'

'Well, good for you. Motivation always helps. I'm sure you *will* do well.' Hope's heart began to thump in her chest. Those days when she'd thought she could do anything. The ones spent with Theo. 'How about you, Willow?'

'I've just bought a car. I've been saving for a while and Dad topped it up so I could afford an electric one. This is the first time I've taken it for more than a few miles. It's outside.'

'I'd be interested to hear what you think of it. I'm considering changing mine.'

Willow nodded. 'It's great, better for the environment. And it'll be handy for going up to see Dad…' She frowned. 'Sorry.'

'What for? You are allowed to mention him, you know.' Hope could bear it. She *had* to bear it.

'I just thought… Dad didn't say anything, but frankly he's pretty transparent most of the time and we know you were dating. We didn't come to pry. We just wanted to know that you're all right. Didn't we, Phoebs?' Phoebe nodded, the two of them looking so downcast that Hope felt suddenly guilty about not telling them the truth.

'It's complicated.'

'Yes, we got that. It often is.' Phoebe summed the situation up neatly.

Hope puffed out a breath, feeling a tear roll down her cheek. That was the one thing she'd promised herself not to do, and now that it had happened almost anything seemed possible.

'Theo and I were good friends. Really good friends. Nothing happened between us…' Maybe Willow should hear that.

'Shame. Perhaps it should've. He might not look quite so lost now.' Willow grimaced.

Too much information. Or…not enough. 'Is he all right?'

'He's good. Likes the new job, although he's working really hard. He gets that break-up look in his eyes every now and then.'

Hope supposed that Willow would recognise that, since she'd seen Theo's break-up with her mother. 'Has he said anything?'

Willow shook her head. 'No, Dad and I don't go into a lot of detail about our relationships. He gets embarrassed…'

Hope suspected that it wasn't a case of embarrassment on Theo's part. 'Or maybe he trusts you?'

Phoebe nodded. 'That's a thought. If you want to see embarrassment then try talking to *my* dad about boyfriends.'

'Well, that's all there is, really. Things didn't work out and I miss him. It'll mend, for both of us.' Hope knew that it wouldn't ever mend for her, but she couldn't think of anything else to say. If life was a series of what-ifs and broken dreams, then she'd keep that to herself.

'Hmm. Platonic affair.' Hope hadn't heard the term before, but Phoebe nodded in agreement with Willow's assessment.

'You think so?'

'I had one last year. It was just like having an affair, only without the…you know.'

'Sex, Willow. You can say it.'

Willow grinned. 'Well, we thought we'd better get around to the *sex*, and… It was a bit of a disaster, really. We kissed a bit but we just weren't feeling the feels, and we ended up going to the pictures, instead.'

Right, then. Nothing like her and Theo. 'At least you had the gumption to do what you really wanted.'

'Yeah, Dad gave me that talk. It's excruciating. He gets so embarrassed. You're not like that.'

Hope had been feeling very old. As if life had passed her by, and she'd never get any of it back again. But she still had some things in common with these young women. She could still feel the feels, and still dance in the dark.

'Good to hear.' She got to her feet. It was time to move on now, from Theo. She'd have plenty of time to think about him later. 'I've saved a few things for you. I don't know whether you can use them for your quilts or not.'

She fetched the cardboard box from the top of

the fridge, putting it onto the table and laying her hand on the flaps at the top to stop Willow and Phoebe from looking inside.

'Here's the thing. If you can use any of this, then please take whatever you want. If you can't, I'm not interested in just passing my junk over to you so you have to deal with it. I can take it down to the charity shop.'

Phoebe nodded. 'Gotcha.'

Willow opened the box, tipping its contents out onto the table. 'What? Don't you want these? They're lovely.'

'It's old costume jewellery, and I don't have a clue where it came from. I'm never going to use any of it, and it doesn't have any sentimental value. Like I said, if you want it, take it, but don't feel you have to.'

Willow nodded, sorting through the collection of old brooches, rings and pendants. 'Look at this one, Phoebs. Very retro.' She held up an enamel pendant that looked as if it came from the nineteen sixties. 'Oh, and look at this. It would be great with your green top. I can use any of this for quilts. I'm getting into adding all kinds of things…'

Examining everything took a while, and by the time they'd finished there was a large pile that Willow wanted to take, and two much smaller piles, one for Phoebe and one for the charity shop. Hope had felt she needed Theo to help her move on, and she had, but this was fun as well.

'I don't suppose… You could stay for dinner if you wanted. If you're not doing anything.'

Willow and Phoebe looked at each other. 'Well…if you don't mind. You still have to try out my car, to see whether you like it.'

Suddenly Hope had everything in common with these young women. 'Stay. I insist. You want some music while we cook?'

Phoebe took out her phone. 'I've got a sixties mix. I can connect with your speakers…'

'Yes, connect away.' Phoebe would have to show her how to do that some time. It didn't look too difficult. Less than a minute later, Phoebe was dancing across to the fridge to inspect its contents.

'You know…' Willow was still sitting with Hope at the kitchen table and clearly had something on her mind. 'Did Dad ever tell you when he adopted me?'

'It was after he married your mother, wasn't it?'

'Yeah, that's when I agreed to it, and they started all the paperwork. It takes a while.'

'Okay.' Hope waited, wondering what on earth Willow wanted to say.

'When Mum left, she left all the papers behind. She'd signed her part and had it witnessed, but Dad hadn't yet. He showed me, and I thought he was going to tear it all up and send me home. But he just wanted to ask me if it was okay for him to sign them.' Willow shrugged. 'The next day we went to the solicitor and that was it. He'd adopted me.'

Tears were never too far away these days, and Hope felt them running down her cheeks. 'Theo didn't want to miss his chance.'

Willow shrugged. 'I don't know about that. I wasn't exactly the perfect child at the time. But the thing is…my dad's the most faithful person I know. He's always stuck by me.'

Hope hugged her. 'That was his privilege, Willow. I wouldn't have expected anything else from him, but thank you for telling me.'

It was something for Hope to remember, if she ever plucked up the courage to see Theo again. Whatever happened, however that worked out, she already knew that she could rely on him to be faithful to his word.

CHAPTER SIXTEEN

THEO WAS AS nervous as a kitten. A very small kitten that had been separated from its mother. It wasn't an emotion that he was all that familiar with, and that unnerved him even more.

He was back in Hastings to finish clearing out the flat before the lease was up and…

Strike that. He was back in Hastings to see Hope. If he couldn't admit to it anyone else, and maybe not even to her, then he had to admit it to himself. Over the last week, he'd mentally prepared for every possible outcome of their meeting so it would be foolish to try to convince himself that this wasn't his purpose.

He parked in the road, outside her house, feeling that he'd probably lost driveway privileges. Kitchen door privileges as well, so he knocked at the front door. Her car was here, but there was no answer.

He was here now. He had nothing to lose, and probably nothing to gain, but he had to see her. Ask one final question—one that wasn't totally impractical this time—and hear her answer. He took the path around the house, stopping suddenly in his tracks as he saw her sitting on the patio, outside the kitchen door.

'Theo!' She almost jumped out of her skin, and he took a step back. She looked so beautiful, her worn jeans and T-shirt covered in grime, and her hair tied up in a colourful scarf. Just exquisite.

'I…um… I was in Hastings anyway…' That wouldn't do. 'I came to see you, Hope. There's something I want to say to you.'

She looked at him thoughtfully. And then suddenly she smiled. 'Then come and sit down. I won't bite you, Theo.'

Maybe she was considering poisoning him, instead. He walked over to her, sitting down opposite her at the small table. Hope was always dazzling, but after five weeks of darkness, it was almost impossible to look at her.

'What do you want to say?' She seemed composed, but her question was almost a whisper. Hope was feeling something, but keeping it to herself. Theo couldn't blame her for that.

'Before that… I want to apologise.'

Genuine surprise flashed in her eyes. 'What for?'

'For leaving. Without saying goodbye.'

'I let you go, without saying goodbye. Doesn't that make us even?'

'Not really. I asked you an impossible question. I see that now.'

She didn't answer, raising the cup of tea beside her to her lips. Theo saw her hand shake, almost spilling it before she took a sip. Hope was holding out on him, and he realised that there *was* something far more hurtful than anger or weeping. Then suddenly, a tear rolled down her cheek.

'Theo, I saw Willow last weekend.'

'You did?' He swallowed hard. 'I mean…good. I'm glad you didn't feel that you shouldn't.'

Hope took a breath. She was holding some emotion in, but Theo couldn't tell what it was. 'We're not as clever as we thought we were. She'd worked out that there was something going on between us. She came to see if I was still talking to her, and I made it quite clear to her that I was. I didn't tell her any of the details and she didn't ask.'

'Thank you. I'd hoped that Willow wouldn't be caught up in this but… I should have known you'd be kind to her.'

'Well, she was kind to me. She told me that you'd finalised her adoption after her mother left—' Theo opened his mouth to ask what else he would have done and Hope held up her hand to silence him. 'She said that you're the most faithful person she knows. I knew that already, but I just needed to be reminded of it. So tell me what you've come to say, Theo. Whatever it is, I'm listening.'

Sudden warmth filled his veins. It was as if his heart had stuttered and then restarted, and he could almost feel his mind clearing itself of all the hurt and pain. Tears started to course down Hope's cheeks, and they came almost as a relief to him. He was prepared for this, and reached into his pocket for a handkerchief.

She wiped her eyes, leaving a smear of dirt on her cheek. Theo took a breath…

'I've been talking too. In broad terms…' He didn't want to give the impression that he'd gone into detail, either. 'Ted.'

She smiled tearily. 'I expect broad terms with Ted is worth about an hour's worth of detail in anyone else's currency. Go on.'

'We want different things, Hope. All kinds of different things. But sometimes you have to look at the one, most important thing that you want. The thing you'd sacrifice everything else for. And my one, important, all-encompassing thing is you.'

She flushed, bright red. 'But…?'

'I have no doubts, and there'll be no regrets. I love you, Hope, and I want to be with you.'

She started to cry again. Anything would be better than this…

'I love you too, Theo. You're my one important thing, and being with you would be the only adventure I ever needed. Can't you see that's why I asked you to go?'

That made no sense. And then suddenly, in a blinding flash of light, it made perfect sense. He wanted only the best for Hope, for her to fulfil her dreams. And she wanted the best for him.

'Because you thought that a job was more important to me than you are?'

She shook her head. 'We could have worked that out. But you still have the opportunity to start another family, Theo. I don't know if I can give you that.'

He could tell her that didn't matter to him. But now was the time for complete honesty, even if it might not be what Hope wanted to hear. 'I can't say that it wouldn't be a disappointment to close that door but... A family isn't just children, it's a loving partnership. You're the one, true love of my life and if it doesn't happen for you then it doesn't happen for me.'

She stared at him. 'You're sure, Theo.'

'I've never been so sure of anything. If the one thing that we both want is to be together, then everything else falls into place.'

'That sounds...' She reached for him, and his whole being trembled in anticipation of her touch. Then suddenly she pulled her hand back, as if she'd realised something. 'I'm all dirty.'

He took her in his arms, kissing her. 'So am I, now.'

They'd spent a long time, kissing out here on the patio. Each time was better than the last, more tender and more exciting. Theo really did know how to kiss a girl.

They both knew that they could wait. Hope was sure of him, and she knew that Theo was sure of her. No more rushing to grab at moments that might not come again. He laughingly enquired exactly why she was so grubby, and Hope took him upstairs.

'Wow! This is an amazing room.' Theo looked around the empty front bedroom. 'You've cleared all of this? Not just put it somewhere else?'

'All of it. I decided that finishing one room would spur me on to do the others. I worked pretty hard at it.' Theo had dark rings under his eyes, and Hope realised that he'd been working much too hard, as well.

'We can take a rest now.' He put his arm around her, bending to kiss her. 'Both of us.'

'I've taken some holiday next week. I was going to clean up in here and give it a coat of paint. Open the shutters and let the light in. I wish it were all done now.' This would be a beautiful room to spend their first night together in.

He smiled down at her. 'I have Monday and Tuesday off work. Ted put me on notice that if I didn't take some of the days owing me, he'd suspend me.'

Hope laughed. 'He wouldn't...would he?'

'He might. I decided not to put up a fight.'

'So, that's four whole days, Theo.'

He nodded. 'I wonder...shall we see which way the wind's blowing? Since the fates seem to be on our side today?'

That would be wonderful. Too much to hope for, maybe. 'You could try. But we might be disappointed.'

There was a light in his eyes as he took his phone from his pocket and dialled. A quick conversation, mostly 'yes' and 'no' and then a 'thank you' didn't tell Hope all that much, and she waited impatiently for him to end the call.

'Well?'

'Shame…' He shot her a solemn look. 'They're booked up this weekend, and all that Denny and Tim can offer us is one room. And a bottle of champagne.'

'Theo!' She launched herself at him in delight, flinging her arms around his neck to kiss him, and he took a step back against the wall. Now the back of his shirt was probably covered in plaster dust.

'We can stay for an extra couple of days if we want, and when we get back we'll set to work on this room. Make each other happy.'

'And if we make a baby, at the same time?' Hope asked him.

He smiled. 'Do we need any other plans? We could just take one day at a time and see what happens.'

'Yes. We'll do that.'

'Only… There's one thing I don't want to leave to chance.' He fell to one knee. That was his trouser leg all dusty now. Then Hope forgot all about that, because he'd taken something from his pocket.

'Will you marry me, Hope? It would be the honour and delight of my life if you said yes.'

It was perfect. Theo always had liked to do everything the right way, and he couldn't have made this moment any better.

'Yes, Theo. I want to marry you more than anything.'

He slipped the ring on her finger. Three diamonds glistened in the light, and she kissed him, tears in her eyes. 'It's so beautiful, Theo. And I love you so much.'

He smiled down at her. 'So you'll run away with me now?'

'I'll follow you anywhere. Only won't you need some clean clothes? I'm all for running away in comfort.'

'I have some at my old flat. The lease isn't up until next week and I only took what I needed when I first moved up to London.'

'Go. I'll be ready by the time you get back.' Hope wondered whether her eagerness might be construed as a little unromantic. 'Am I rushing too much?'

He hushed her, kissing the finger that bore his ring. 'We have a future now, Hope. It means more than anything to me that you can't wait to get started on it.'

Waking up in the room by the sea was nice. Waking up in Theo's arms was the best thing in the world.

'Awake?' His fingers moved against her skin, and she shivered.

'You haven't been watching me sleep again, have you?' She moved against him, feeling their bodies easing together in that sweet synchronicity that seemed to govern every part of their lives.

'No, you made your views on that very clear last night. I was listening to you sleep.'

'That's worse, Theo.' She snuggled against his chest, and he kissed the top of her head.

'Did I make you happy?'

'Very happy. Several times. Did I make you happy?'

He chuckled. 'You need to ask?'

No. Hope didn't need to ask. She'd known that Theo would be an amazing lover and he was a generous one too, sharing everything with her. 'I'm going to hold you to all of those promises you made.'

'I'm counting on you to do just that.'

They both jumped as a knock sounded on the door. Then Theo chuckled. 'I'm pretty sure no one's stabbed themselves. It's half past ten, so that'll be breakfast.' He got out of bed, grinning at her as she unashamedly watched him walk across the room, to fetch his dressing gown.

He opened the door, looking outside, and Tim's voice floated into the room. 'Sorry to disturb, lovebirds.'

'Thanks, Tim,' Theo called back along the corridor, then wheeled the breakfast trolley into the room, closing the door.

He slung the dressing gown onto a chair, coming back to the bed. Hope loved the way that Theo was so comfortable in his skin, so unaware of his gorgeous nakedness. She was becoming less self-conscious of hers, because he never failed to tell her how beautiful she was.

'So what's on the agenda for today?' she asked, pouring the coffee as he slid back beneath the bed covers.

'Umm. Some romantic fossil hunting? Romantic walks around the island...' Hope's phone beeped as Theo elaborated on the list.

'Ah. First we'll have to do some romantic texting.' She scrolled through the text that Willow had just sent. 'Apparently Willow tried both our mobiles, yesterday evening, and then tried us both at home. Then she called your parents this morning, to see if you'd gone over there to see them, and your mother told her that you'd mentioned you were taking this weekend off because you were going down to Hastings...' Hope scrolled a little further. 'Where are we? What are we doing?'

'Ah. Is she all right?'

'Yes, she says she's texting me because you might fly into a panic and wonder whether she's all right. You're not panicking, are you?'

Theo shook his head. 'I'm just enquiring. Are you going to text her back?'

'What do I say? In Dorset. Having sex.'

Theo snorted with laughter. 'Not quite how I'd

put it. I'd go for Romantic engagement weekend. That way she can decide for herself what we're doing.'

'She knows what we're doing, Theo. How's this for a compromise?' Hope started to type.

Having romantic engagement sex...

'She's going to call...' Theo chuckled, sipping his coffee.

'No, she isn't.' Hope sent the text, reaching for one of the warm croissants. Her phone beeped again, and Theo picked it up. 'What does she say?'

Delighted scream. Catch you both later.

Theo nodded. 'That works for me.'

'Me too. Did I just lie to your daughter? We're actually having breakfast.'

'No.' Theo put his coffee to one side, and took Hope's croissant from her hand. 'Romantic engagement sex sounds like a fine way to start the day...'

EPILOGUE

Three years later

'HOME.' THEO GOT out of the car, taking their two-year-old son, Jack, from his car seat. Next to Jack was the carrycot with their newborn baby girl, just two days old and sleeping peacefully.

'Home, Daddy!' Jack took his father's hand, craning to see his little sister as Theo walked him slowly to the front door, the carrycot in his other hand. One more view of Theo's back that Hope couldn't resist.

Willow's car drew up behind them, and she jumped from the driver's seat, sprinting across to Hope to help her out of the car.

'Thanks, I can manage.' Hope grinned at her. 'You might want to go and help your dad out.'

Willow whirled round. 'Dad! Freeze!' she called after Theo, just as he executed a deft manoeuvre that allowed him to keep hold of Jack and his little sister and open the front door, all at the same time.

'Managing,' Theo called back. 'Why don't you give Hope a hand?'

Willow rolled her eyes. 'Make up your minds, people!'

'Sorry, sweetheart.' Hope shot her an apologetic look. 'If you could bring my bag in, that would be a real help...'

The house really *was* a home, now. The first floor was full of light, instead of boxes, and housed their own bedroom along with a room each for Jack and the baby, a guest room and a good-sized office for the two days a week that Theo worked from home. Downstairs the two bedrooms had gone back to their original purpose, a dining room and a TV room. It was a place they both loved, and would always come back to, full of memories and hopes for the future.

Theo had planted several trees in the back garden, which would be tall enough for them to sit beneath in twenty years' time. And the large oak table that Theo's parents had bought them, as a wedding present, had developed a few small scuffs courtesy of their son and would no doubt gather up a few more when their daughter got a little older.

Coming back home was always special, because Theo had made sure they went away to special places too. They'd been to Japan for their honeymoon, and to Venice for Jack's first birthday. Last Christmas had been spent in Canada and they'd travelled the length and breadth of the British Isles, sometimes going with Theo for work trips, and sometimes for short holidays.

Hope had decided to give up work when Jack was born, wanting to spend as much time as she could with him until he started school. That had opened up new horizons, too, and her work with several different local organisations had led to her becoming a trustee of a medical charity for children. Speaking on their behalf had been nerve-racking at first, but Theo had supported her all the way and Hope had derived a deep satisfaction from her role in heightening awareness and raising funds. He'd encouraged Hope to write a children's storybook too, which Willow was illustrating. Theo had been right. They'd both taken the one thing that they really wanted, and everything else had followed.

Hope was chivvied upstairs and ordered to rest, and Theo carried the baby up and put her into the crib next to the bed. Willow took charge of Jack, and Theo brought Hope a cup of tea.

'What are they doing down there?'

Theo sank down onto the bed next to her. 'They're in the garden. Willow's dancing and Jack's running.'

'Good. Next time just freeze when she tells you, eh?'

Theo leaned back onto the pillows, his hands behind his head and a besotted grin on his face. 'I had it all worked out. Jack and I practised with his stuffed giraffe.'

'You used a stuffed giraffe to stand in for our daughter?' Hope nudged her elbow into his ribs in mock horror.

'Jack insisted. Who am I to argue?'

'You're such a softie, Theo.' Hope leaned over to kiss him. 'That's why I love you so much. Have you thought any more about a name?'

'What do you think of Clara?'

'Mum's middle name?' Hope leaned over towards the crib, calling the name softly, and the baby's eyes opened suddenly.

'You're not humouring me at all. She didn't just react to the sound of your voice.' Theo chuckled. 'Clara's a lovely choice of name. I think she's definitely a Clara. Thank you for thinking of it.'

Theo propped himself on his elbow, looking at little Clara. 'Are we going to stop now? We have so much more than we ever dreamed we would.'

'Yes. I think so.' Hope's second pregnancy had been a little harder than the first, and she knew that Theo had been worried at times. 'There are lots more adventures waiting for us.'

'Yeah. I was thinking that, too.'

Hope fed Clara, and then Theo rocked her back to sleep. Then Willow appeared in the doorway, holding Jack's hand. 'He wants to come and say hello.'

Theo nodded, beckoning to Jack and lifting him up onto his lap. Willow gave a wrapped package to Hope.

'Is this what I think it is?' Hope opened the parcel, holding up the quilt that was inside. 'That's beautiful, Willow, thank you so much. We've decided on a name for her. It's Clara—what do you think?'

'I like it.' Willow grinned. 'Can I have a picture? Of you all.' She took her phone from her pocket.

'Don't you mean of *us* all? Come here.'

Clara was wrapped in her quilt and put into Hope's arms. Theo shifted so that Willow could sit in between them, and Jack slid over onto her lap. Theo held the phone out, his other arm around Willow's shoulders. Their family. Brought together by chance and held together by love.

* * * * *

If you enjoyed this story,
check out these other great reads from
Annie Claydon

Neurosurgeon's IVF Mix-Up Miracle
Winning Over the Off-Limits Doctor
Country Fling with the City Surgeon
Healed by Her Rival Doc

All available now!

HARLEQUIN
Reader Service

Enjoyed your book?

Try the perfect subscription for Romance readers and get more great books like this delivered right to your door.

See why over 10+ million readers have tried Harlequin Reader Service.

Start with a Free Welcome Collection with free books and a gift—valued over $20.

Choose any series in print or ebook. See website for details and order today:

TryReaderService.com/subscriptions